There were things that he and Caitlin had to talk about.

Things they had to sort out. And this time he was keeping his head!

All right, admit it, he told himself furiously—the real phrase he needed was that this time he was *thinking* with his head. This time he wasn't going to let his most basic instincts get in the way of rational thought—the calm approach was what he needed.

The problem was Caitlin. Five minutes spent with her and he forgot the control and experience he had learned after thirty-two years of living. One look at those eyes, the curves of her body, and he reverted to the yearning hunger of an adolescent who had just discovered his sexuality and the attractions of the opposite sex.

And he didn't like the way that made him feel.

EXPECTING!

She's sexy,
successful...
and
PREGNANT!

Relax and enjoy our fabulous series about
couples whose passion ends in
pregnancies...sometimes unexpected!
Of course, the birth of a baby is always a
joyful event, and we can guarantee that our
characters will become wonderful moms
and dads—but what happened in
those nine months before?

Share the surprises, emotions, drama and
suspense as our parents-to-be come to terms
with the prospect of bringing a new baby
into the world. All will discover that the
business of making babies brings with it
the most special love of all....

Coming next month:

His Pregnancy Ultimatum
by Helen Bianchin #2433

Delivered only by Harlequin Presents®

Kate Walker

THEIR SECRET BABY

EXPECTING!

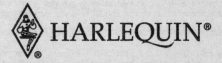

HARLEQUIN®

TORONTO • NEW YORK • LONDON
AMSTERDAM • PARIS • SYDNEY • HAMBURG
STOCKHOLM • ATHENS • TOKYO • MILAN • MADRID
PRAGUE • WARSAW • BUDAPEST • AUCKLAND

ISBN 0-373-12432-5

THEIR SECRET BABY

First North American Publication 2004.

www.eHarlequin.com

Printed in U.S.A.

CHAPTER ONE

RHYS MORGAN swung his car off the main road and pressed his foot down on the accelerator as even the powerful engine slowed on the steep slope before it.

'*This* is the road to a hotel?' he muttered impatiently to himself, steering the sleek vehicle carefully around the wicked bends with hands that were clenched so tightly around the wheel the knuckles showed white. 'It's more likely to put people off.'

But nothing would deter him. Not now.

Not when the end of his search was finally in sight. When the prospect of coming face to face with the woman he had finally tracked down seemed only seconds away. When he could finally learn from her the whereabouts of the one thing on which his thoughts had centred to the exclusion of everything else.

His daughter.

He had neglected his work, his business, his friends—his life for the past three months, because of this. He had travelled for miles, taking in at least three countries and God knew how many towns. And all because of one small person who he had never known existed until months after her birth.

The child he had thought would never be born. The child he'd thought his estranged wife would have been determined to destroy, because she had always said pregnancy would ruin both her figure and her lifestyle.

But just three months ago he had learned that something very different had happened.

The steep drive flattened out suddenly to a wide gravel-covered parking space, at the end of which stood the small, family-run hotel he had come to find.

Set high above the valley, it stood square and solid against the driving rain, with the wild hills and the deep expanse of Lake Windermere spread out below it.

'At last!'

Rhys steered the car into a roughly marked parking space and pulled on the brakes, sitting back with a deep sigh. Staring through the sheeting rain with his sapphire-blue eyes narrowed, he pushed both hands through the sleek blackness of his hair and frowned in thoughtful concentration.

He was here.

And it was time to consider his next move.

Time to decide exactly how he was going to play things when he finally came face to face with his wife's cousin. Caitlin Richardson. The woman who now had custody of the daughter he had never known he had.

Caitlin Richardson put the phone down and sighed wearily, pushing one hand through the dark fall of her hair. She grimaced as she felt how rough and uneven the ends had become. She hadn't had time to have a decent haircut in weeks.

She hadn't had time for anything.

Caring for a six-month-old baby didn't leave much time for leisure or relaxation—or looking after yourself for that matter. Not when it was combined with trying to hold down a full-time job and earn enough money to feed them both as well.

And she was tired. Worn out. Fleur had been sleeping badly for the last couple of weeks—a combination of teething and the change in her routine—and as a result Caitlin herself hadn't had a full night's rest in as long as she could remember.

Certainly not since the news had come through about Amelie and Josh.

'No!'

It was a low, drawn-out moan. She rubbed the back of her hand over eyes shadowed with the darkness of misery as memories she wished she could erase surfaced to hit her in the face, making her close her eyes against the pain.

'I don't want to remember.'

'I'm sorry?'

It was a stranger's voice. A voice she had never heard before, and it broke into her thoughts in a rush, startling her and jolting her eyes wide open.

'I—I was talking to myself.'

It was difficult to collect her thoughts. Almost impossible when she found herself staring into eyes as brilliant and stunning a blue as these.

And to have been caught talking to herself! Talking to herself about things she didn't even want to think about privately, let alone bring out into the open in front of a total stranger! It was not in the least bit surprising that all coherent thought had fled her mind.

Fortunately, years of training and a determined professionalism snapped into place, giving her at least *something* to say.

'Can I help you?'

She hoped her smile was convincing. Hoped that she at least looked welcoming, if he was a guest.

Was he a guest? He didn't look the sort of person who normally came to the Linford. Casual family groups, or retired couples who were having a weekend away, were more the sort of clientele who favoured this far from five-star hotel, especially in a cold, damp spring like this one.

This man looked too affluent for them. For all that he was so casually dressed, in tight-fitting black jeans and an oatmeal-coloured sweater, his clothes had a style and a quality to them that spoke of money, and plenty of it.

'I have a reservation...'

So he *was* a guest. Somehow she managed to swallow down the exclamation of surprise that almost escaped her and reached for the computer keyboard.

'In what name?'

'Delaney—Matthew Delaney.'

Had he moved forward? He suddenly seemed too close for comfort. She felt the tiny hairs on her skin prickle and lift in apprehension, for no good reason that she could think of.

'Delaney...'

Her vision blurred as she hunted for the name on the screen. She had never been so intensely aware of another human being in her life.

Those eyes really were stunning. Deep, deep blue, like the sky at the end of a long, hot summer day, just before night. He too needed a haircut and the fall of his dark hair over his high forehead was a sensual temptation in itself. Her fingers itched to brush it back, to feel the warmth of his skin under their tips.

'Delaney...' she tried again, more forceful this time, concentrating ferociously.

Then jumped nervously as a long, square-tipped finger moved past her and stabbed purposefully on a computer key.

'What—?'

'Matthew Delaney.'

His tone sounded reasonable enough but there was a note threaded through it that set her teeth on edge even if she didn't quite know why.

'My name—it's right there.'

'I could see that!'

The need not to look a fool made her voice sharper than she would have liked—and sharper than *he* liked too, that much was obvious, as the straight black brows twitched together at her tone.

'I'm sorry—I mean…'

'What you mean is, keep my nose out.'

To her relief his voice sounded reasonable, even amused, and a faint smile softened the hard, controlled line of his mouth.

'Well, I wouldn't have put it quite that bluntly. But I did have things in hand.'

'Of course you did, Miss—' those blue eyes dropped to the name badge pinned to her smart white blouse '—Miss Richardson.'

And suddenly, unnervingly, the smile had vanished as swiftly as it had come.

'So now that you have things in hand, Ms Caitlin Richardson, would you like to tell me exactly where my room is?'

This Caitlin Richardson was not at all what he had expected, Rhys reflected. He'd never seen her before. She hadn't been one of the few guests Amelie had invited to their whirlwind wedding just over two years before. Knowing she was related to Amelie, he had expected her to look like his ex-wife. And when you were anticipating the sleek, blonde, sophisticated, Parisian style of Amelie Deslonge, then this very ordinary little creature was something of a shock to the system.

Average height; average build; average colouring. That was the way he had described her within the privacy of his own thoughts. There was simply nothing special about her…

Or, rather, nothing until she had opened her eyes. And one swift, astounded glance into their golden depths had told a very different story.

He had never seen eyes like those. Cat's eyes. Huge, golden, glowing eyes, fringed with impossibly long lashes.

Stunning eyes.

Beautiful.

Bedroom eyes.

And suddenly his thoughts were off course, on very different tracks from the ones on which they had been running as he had come up the drive, walked through the door.

'Room three-four-two. If you'd just sign here, and put your car's registration there…'

'Of course.'

Damn it! The distraction of his thoughts had almost led him to sign automatically, using his *real* name!

It took a hasty second's pause to reconsider and turn his pen to a slightly different angle before he managed to scribble down the fake identity he had used to make his booking.

Well, not totally false, he admitted to himself. He was entitled to every part of it. Just not in that order. Matthew and Delaney were his middle names, the Delaney coming from his mother's maiden name.

It might make things a little complicated when it came to paying the bill, but by then he hoped to have made his real identity clear anyway. But Rhys Matthew Delaney Morgan might have been too well known to Caitlin Richardson, or anyone who knew of his reputation as an international art dealer, alerting her to the fact that her cousin's estranged husband was on his way to the hotel, determined to find some facts and get some answers to some very serious questions.

Answers that only Caitlin Richardson could give.

'You're on the top floor. The lift is over there—the staircase is just around the corner to your right. Would you like any help with your luggage?'

'Hardly.'

He indicated the one small bag that stood on the polished wooden floor at his feet with a casual nod. To a man of his height and strength, it was a featherweight, no trouble at all.

'I think I can manage.'

The irony in his tone brought hot colour rushing up into her cheeks, emphasising the high bones, the soft skin.

'I'm quite sure you can!'

Once again the sharp edge to her words revealed how uncomfortable she felt.

She'd feel a whole lot more uncomfortable if she knew who he really was, Rhys reflected darkly. If she suspected the truth of his real identity and the reason why he was here, she was more than likely to snatch back the proffered key, grabbing it away from him and refusing to let him touch it.

'Breakfast is from seven…'

The practised list of details slid right over his head as a sudden, disturbing thought struck him. He recalled how, as he had walked from the car park to the main entrance to the hotel, he had watched the sheep grazing peacefully on the slopes of the hills outside. Now he had the distinctly unnerving feeling that he was in the position of being the big, bad wolf, circling the unsuspecting lambs, waiting for a chance to pounce.

It wasn't a position he was used to being in. Or one that he had ever thought to find himself taking. It was so alien to him that he scarcely recognised himself.

'And if you want anything in your room, then the room-service menu is available twenty-four hours a day. I think that's everything.'

'Not quite.'

'Oh?'

Once again that puzzled frown crossed her face.

'What else is there?'

'When do you get off duty?'

Hell and damnation! How had that slipped past his guard? OK, so, ultimately, that had been part of the plan. To get to know her, win her trust. Then to ask her out—to wine and dine her, and try to tease the information he needed out of her without her knowing.

Then he would have declared his true identity and if necessary gone for the big guns—by bringing in his lawyers.

But now he'd risked messing it all up by blundering in way too soon. What had he been thinking?

No, he admitted to himself drily. The question was what had he been thinking *with*? And the answer was most definitely not his brain.

Looking into those stunning tawny eyes, he saw the polite smile, the helpful expression fade from them rapidly and knew that he'd blundered. In his haste to get closer to knowing the truth, he'd risked taking several steps backwards instead of forward.

'Off duty?' Caitlin echoed, realising that it was a phrase she hadn't actually used about herself in a long time.

'I wondered if you'd like a drink, or a meal...'

Just for a second some tiny, irresponsible and young part of her heart, a part she hadn't felt since she had learned the truth about Josh, lifted at the thought. When had she last really been 'off duty'?

And when had some attractive stranger last asked her out on an impulse?

But of course it couldn't be.

'I'm sorry. It's not possible, I'm afraid. The management don't encourage staff to socialise with guests. Policy…'

Policy be blowed! she added privately. If her father knew about the invitation then he'd be there like a shot, urging her to accept, to go out and have some fun. To remember she was only twenty-four.

He would even volunteer to babysit, she was sure.

But then her father didn't know the real truth about Amelie and Josh. He knew nothing of the sense of betrayal, the shock and loss that had torn through her when she had found out.

Everyone thought she was still mourning Josh and Amelie. They didn't know that she had lost them both months before the actual accident. Before Fleur had even been born.

'Are you sure?'

Something had changed, Caitlin thought uneasily. It was as if that easy smile was fraying at the edges, the warmth in his eyes cooling rapidly. And without that warmth, they were very cold indeed.

Some instinct she couldn't explain had her pressing the bell under the desk to summon the porter, the need to have company suddenly uppermost in her mind.

'It's only a drink I'm offering. Nothing to be afraid of.'

Caitlin chose to ignore the deliberate provocation of that remark.

'I'm quite sure. But thank you for asking anyway.'

'No problem.'

She did a good line in polite regret, Rhys admitted. So much so that he almost believed her himself.

Almost.

But the investigations that had got him here today had been too thorough to allow him to be convinced. The so-called 'management' was her father, who owned the hotel.

And if Bob Richardson's daughter was anything like her late cousin Amelie, then she could twist any susceptible male around her little finger and still not have a hair out of place.

Hadn't she already done so with him? Driving him to forget his carefully thought-out plans and make a totally uncharacteristic impulsive move.

But how had she done it?

Two minutes ago he had thought her ordinary. Compared with Amelie, she *was* ordinary. Then something had happened. Something he couldn't put his finger on or explain.

But one thing he knew for sure was that the process of finding out about the baby suddenly seemed to be a much more attractive prospect than he had ever anticipated.

'Caitlin?'

It was another voice. A masculine voice, but lighter and more youthful than his own, bringing his eyes to the door where the tall, gangling figure of a young porter had suddenly appeared.

'Did you want something?'

'Yes.'

Caitlin nodded her dark head.

'Mr—Mr Delaney needs his bag taken up to his room. Three-four-two.'

'I—' Rhys began, but then a glance into the golden eyes of the woman before him made him clamp down sharply on the protest he had been about to make.

There was defiance in those eyes, defiance and a touch of wary challenge. And a determination not to back down.

He'd acted unthinkingly, stupidly, jumping in too fast, and by doing so had alerted her suspicions in a way that was the last thing he needed. He wanted to win her over, not have her alarmed and ready to fight.

And so he forced himself to smile and nod too, turning

his gaze to the porter, and inclining his head in the direction of his case.

'Thank you.'

'Sean will take you to your room.' It was icily polite. Dismissive.

He could almost feel her eyes on him as the porter came forward, lifting the case with an ease that made a mockery of the suggestion that Rhys should need his help at all. He was inches taller than the younger man—broader too at every point that mattered, with clearly defined muscles under the clinging sweater.

'This way, sir.'

The words were cut through by a sound. A sudden and totally unexpected sound that rang through the stiffly awkward silence in the reception hall, bringing everyone's head up.

It was the cry of a very young child.

And it came from the door behind Caitlin Richardson. The door that led straight into the receptionist's office.

The baby.

Rhys couldn't stop himself. Reacting totally instinctively, he had paused and half turned, sharply assessing eyes going swiftly in the direction of the sound, before he realised how stupid he was being. How much he was giving away.

No! he forced his mind to scream at his wayward body. Not now! Not yet!

Somehow he managed to rein in the automatic rush forward, to push the door open, gather the child in his arms.

'Not yet! Not yet!' he muttered under his breath. 'It's too damn soon!'

Luckily Caitlin had also reacted immediately, whirling round and hurrying away, disappearing through the dividing door before he had time to think any further. And Rhys could only be grateful that the speed of her own reaction had meant that she hadn't noticed his own betraying movement.

Hot waves of anger flooded his mind, blending dangerously with emotional pain and an almost unbearable yearning that he could scarcely control. The explosive combination drove out all rational thought, leaving him with just feeling.

Behind that door was his baby. *His* child. And this woman—this *stranger* was in there now with his daughter. It would be her hands that lifted the baby, her arms that held it, her voice that soothed...

'Sir? Mr Delaney?'

The porter's discreet cough, his careful murmur, dragged his thoughts unwillingly back to the present and the need to display a reasonable, uninvolved mask to the hotel staff if they were not to become suspicious. At least for now.

'I'm sorry.'

He switched on an easy smile, turned and forced himself to stroll towards the lift doors.

'Is it usual to bring a baby to work?' he asked as they began their journey upwards.

'Ah, well, that's Miss Caitlin's little girl,' Sean told him. 'Things are rather difficult there.'

Too damn right they were! And the baby was *not* Miss Caitlin's anything...

Rhys swallowed down the angry retort with an effort and opted instead for a casual, man-to-man approach.

'She's an attractive woman.'

'Mmm.' Sean's response was noncommittal. 'But it's look but don't touch where she's concerned. I've only been here just over a month, and I soon learned that!'

'The ice-maiden sort, huh?'

'And how. This is our floor. It's the third door on the left.'

So the youthful Sean had tried it on with Ms Richardson and been rebuffed, Rhys reflected when, left alone, he had tossed his case on the bed and looked around the room that was to be his for the next week or so. Decorated in dark green and white, it seemed clean and comfortable but rather small, even for one person.

But then of course he was used to much better hotels than this. Travelling as often as he did, looking for items to display in his gallery, paintings to sell, he always insisted on the best that money could buy. And his money could buy the very best.

Tossing his keys from one hand to the other, he prowled around the limited space, pausing to stare out of the window. The room was at the back of the hotel, looking out onto the rain-soaked, curving lawn, the dripping greenery of the shrubbery.

And Ms Richardson was an ice maiden. Well, with a little persuasion ice could melt. It was only ice—not stone. And he had plenty of experience of melting reluctant, cool women. It was a challenge, and he'd always liked a challenge.

And she wasn't indifferent to him; he was sure of that. He'd seen the flare of response in her eyes, watched the burn of awareness flood her skin. She might act all cool and collected, but if she was anything like her cousin, like Amelie, then there was a wild volcano underneath, just waiting to break through the layer of ice that covered the surface.

'So, Ms Caitlin Richardson—it's look but don't touch, is it? Well, we shall see.'

As he spoke her name aloud he saw again in his mind the image of her face, of those golden eyes when she had looked at him downstairs. He thought back over the conversation they'd had—calm and businesslike on the surface but whirling with undercurrents and studded with rocks underneath. The things that had been said without a word being spoken.

Had she guessed anything? The atmosphere had been tense, taut enough to stretch the nerves. He'd been a fool to blunder in with his impulsive invitation. Moving too quickly, too thoughtlessly.

He'd better be careful because that impulse had made her wary. With her head up like that and the big tawny eyes wide in something close to alarm, she'd looked as nervous as a young roe deer scenting intruders into her territory. If he didn't take care she'd suspect something.

'Softly, softly…' he murmured to himself.

But even as he resolved on caution, the memory of the moment that he had heard the baby's cry seared into his mind, making his hand clench tight on the keys until the hard metal dug into the skin of his palm. Recalling how she had left the desk and gone into the back room, he found that suddenly he couldn't see, couldn't think for the red mist of anger that hazed his eyes.

That was *his* child, *his* daughter. But he knew nothing about her. He didn't even know her name, goddammit! If he hadn't met up with a mutual friend of his and Amelie's, who had told him the whole story, he would never even have known that the baby existed. His wife had been adamant that children were not for her; that if she got pregnant she would have an immediate abortion.

But somehow Amelie had changed her mind. The baby he'd thought he'd never have was real. And *she*—this Caitlin Richardson, with her cool smile and her cool voice and her 'touch me not' image—was keeping the child from him. She hadn't even let him know. Wouldn't have told him about it if he'd asked.

'Oh, yes, Ms Caitlin Richardson,' he muttered savagely, thudding his clenched fist hard against the edge of the wooden window frame, 'you do right to be wary where I'm concerned. And if you're wise, you'll keep on being wary—much good may it do you! Because I'm going to get my daughter from you whatever it takes. That baby is going to be mine—by fair means or foul.'

And right now, with hot fury blurring his thought processes, quite frankly he felt that *foul* was much the preferable option.

In fact, remembering those burning, molten tawny eyes and the lure of the promises they offered, in total contrast to the frosty control of her ice-maiden act, he thought it was possible that it might be the most enjoyable approach as well.

CHAPTER TWO

THREE days could change so very much, Caitlin reflected as she settled the baby in the office behind the reception desk and prepared for work.

Three days ago, life had seemed settled and controlled. OK, so it was not what she'd wanted, what she *dreamed* of, but after the chaos and misery of the past months it had at last seemed back on some sort of regular track so that she had an idea of where she was going.

But that was before Matthew Delaney had appeared to complicate things.

Oh, be honest! a critical little voice inside her head carped. It's not Matthew Delaney that's complicating things! It's your reaction to him.

'Sleep tight, Fleur, darling.' She used the crooned words to distract herself from her uncomfortable and unwanted thoughts. 'I'll just be right here.'

She didn't want to think about the way that Matthew Delaney suddenly seemed to have become so totally present in her life. She didn't seem to be able to get away from him. If she turned around, he was there, in the hall, in the lounge, in the dining room. Over the three days her feeling of being faintly flattered had changed to one of vague uneasiness, shading into a definite shiver of apprehension whenever she thought of him.

And always, at the back of everything, was this intense awareness of him as a man.

Her skin prickled when he was near. Her heart thudded heavily and every sense seemed heightened, sharpened, in the most disturbing way. She felt intensely feminine, shockingly sensual in a way she had never known. And she couldn't stop her gaze from sliding towards him, fixing on him whenever he was in the room.

A cold chill of uncertainty slid down her spine as she recalled the number of times that he had seemed to sense her eyes on him and looked up, their gazes clashing, fixing, holding for long, disturbing seconds before she had lost her nerve and looked away again sharply.

But that wasn't going to happen again, she resolved, pulling on her tailored navy jacket and smoothing down the matching skirt. She wasn't going to let Matthew Delaney get to her in any way any more.

Her resolve lasted just as long as it took her to leave the office and go to the reception desk.

The flower lay on the polished wooden surface. A single lush, perfect, long-stemmed rose, its rich red colouring proclaiming a message of love to anyone who was interested.

Caitlin was *not* interested.

She was shaken—and unnerved—and furious at being made to feel this way.

And evidence of just who was responsible for putting her in this mood wasn't hard to find.

Matthew Delaney—of course it was Matthew Delaney!—was sitting just a few feet away, relaxing in a huge velvet-covered armchair, hidden behind the pages of a broadsheet morning paper.

'Damn him!' Caitlin muttered under her breath, struggling for control. 'Damn, damn, damn him!'

Couldn't he take no for an answer? Didn't he realise that his attentions and his invitation to dinner weren't welcome? Didn't he—?

But no. She had to collect herself, get herself back under control.

Count to ten.

'One—two—three…'

The final number ten came, and was passed—and came again—and still she couldn't calm down.

And matters were only made so much worse by *that man's* obvious total relaxation.

As she watched, another of the hotel's guests went past his chair and obviously said something. Delaney raised his dark head, responding briefly and lightly. The next moment the sound of his laughter came across the room to where she stood.

She knew that he wasn't laughing at her. Every ounce of common sense she possessed told her that, and yet somehow that laughter sparked off a reaction in her that she couldn't control.

She didn't *want* Matthew Delaney in her life! She didn't want any man! She wanted Josh back. Wanted things to be how they had once been. And she couldn't have that.

Even if Josh were still alive, then things could never be how they had once been. Josh was gone. And Matthew Delaney…

Anger flared, her hold on her temper failing under the impact of the terrible pain that gripped her. Snatching up the red rose, she marched round the desk, across the hall.

'I don't want this!' she declared, throwing it furiously over the top of his paper and down into his lap. 'I don't want anything from you, can't you see that? What do I have to do to get the message across to you?'

His sudden, frozen silence was disturbing, a tiny shiver of apprehension crossing her skin as she saw the way that his hands tightened sharply on the newspaper. Swallowing hard, she nerved herself for the coming storm, half anticipating it with a perverse degree of pleasure.

At least maybe now he would leave her alone.

But then he lowered the newspaper and looked her straight in the face.

And the fact that the deep blue eyes were brimming with an unholy amusement was the last thing she had expected. The glint of wicked mockery stole her breath away and left her standing, unable to speak, shifting uneasily from one foot to another.

'My, we do overreact, don't we?' he drawled. 'It's only a flower—just a—'

'I know very well what it is!' Caitlin flung at him, goaded back into speech by that taunting smile. 'I know it's a rose—but I don't want it! I don't want *anything*! Not from you! I don't want your invitations and your flowers and—'

'I didn't give it to you,' Rhys inserted quietly when she paused for breath.

'What?'

She couldn't believe what she was hearing.

'I didn't give it to you.'

His smile was lethal, totally destroying what little was left of her composure. And what made it all the worse was the fact that it was so gently tolerant—at least on the surface.

'But you must have done! I mean—who else...?'

It was working, Rhys reflected, watching her struggle for breath, trying to find the right words. And about time too.

When she had rejected his invitation to dinner or a drink he had wondered if he'd overstepped the mark, moving too quickly. He was prepared to take this one step at a time, but his patience was limited. If he didn't get to see his daughter, hold his baby in his arms *fast* then he felt that he would implode, unable to contain his feelings any longer.

So instead of pushing, he'd tried the opposite approach.

He would carry on as usual, not saying a word. Not even

directing a glance her way—though when he had looked up several times to see her eyes on him, it had been all he could do not to respond.

But the policy of ignoring her had started to work. He had felt those golden eyes burning into him more and more often over the past forty-eight hours, though her gaze had skittered away nervously whenever he'd looked up.

And now here she was. Nervous and edgy—and shockingly angry—but at last she had come to him.

And the anger wasn't anything to do with him.

'Who else?'

Wary of revealing too much, he dropped his eyes to the rose that still lay in his lap, studying it with a concentrated attention that hid the almost irresistible urge to let his mouth twitch into a triumphant grin.

'Surely you must have guessed?'

'No, I haven't. I don't—*who*?' she almost begged, clearly coming to the end of what little patience she had in reserve.

Rhys reached for the rose, picking it up carefully by the long green, dethorned stem and twirling it round and round reflectively between finger and thumb.

'Your secret admirer,' he murmured softly, glancing upwards from eyes half-veiled by thick black lashes to watch the effect his words had.

They had every bit of the effect he could have wanted.

'Secret admirer!'

It was expelled on a hiss of disbelief, and as if the sigh had been the air escaping from a pricked balloon she subsided rapidly onto a nearby chair, not seeming to trust her legs to keep her upright any more.

'What secret admirer? I thought—'

Hastily she bit the words back, but not quickly enough

to hide the fact that she was betraying something she didn't want him to know.

'You thought that *I* was your admirer,' he supplied as the fiery colour flooded her face and the words faltered on her lips.

'I—I...'

'Well, you could be right.'

He made it sound as if he was putting her out of her misery.

'But you must know that I'm not the only one.'

That brought those brilliant eyes to his face in a rush, wide and darkly clouded with confusion. She looked so bewildered that for a moment he almost felt sorry for her.

Almost.

But then he remembered what she had done to him. The tiny, vulnerable little secret baby that she must know was his and yet was deliberately keeping from him, and his heart hardened until it felt like a lump of stone in his chest.

'I don't—who else?'

'I'm not sure I should betray his secret.'

But he'd pushed her just an inch too far. He saw that from the flash of anger in her eyes, the rejection etched onto her face.

'You don't know, do you?' she stormed, getting back to her feet in a rush. 'You're just pretending! In fact, I don't believe there is any such thing as a ''secret admirer''! You're making it up!'

He hadn't thought of doing any such thing, but it might almost have been worth it if he had. She looked spectacular when she was angry, with those amber eyes blazing and for once a touch of colour across her high cheekbones. And the way she stood, with her hands on her hips in defiance, pushed her small, pert breasts forward in a display that any red-blooded man would appreciate. Especially from this angle.

'And why would I do that?'

'Oh, how should I know? I've no idea what's going on inside that devious head of yours! Just because I turned down your invitation to dinner…'

'Who's turning down dinner invitations?'

Another voice broke into her tirade, obviously with the intent of cooling and calming the atmosphere. Caitlin's father's voice, Rhys recognised at once. Bob Richardson had come up behind her unexpectedly and now he was standing just at her side.

'Oh, nothing…' she muttered, unwilling to continue the conversation, but Rhys wasn't going to let her escape that easily.

'I invited your daughter to dinner but she declined. Said it was policy for staff not to see guests.'

'Cait?'

Caitlin groaned inwardly, knowing just what was coming. She was right.

'What are you talking about? You know there's no such—'

'It wasn't a serious invitation, Dad!'

She knew that look and would do anything to erase it from his face. That 'You need to get out more—have some fun. You're only young' look had appeared at least once a day, if not more, ever since the news about Amelie and Josh had broken.

'What makes you say that?'

Rhys was folding his newspaper, putting it aside as he got to his feet. His smooth, lithe movements, imposing height and a certain intensity in the brilliant blue eyes gave Caitlin the uncomfortable feeling that it was like watching some deadly snake uncoiling, ready to strike.

'What makes you think I wasn't serious?'

'Well—I—you...'

Oh, to blazes with it! She was going to tell him the truth!

'Well, you can hardly say that you seemed disappointed!'

No, that had been a mistake. A big mistake! The gleam in his eye brightened, warning her that she'd fallen into some subtle trap she hadn't even been aware that he'd laid, and cold fingers of doubt crept over her skin.

'I was serious,' he said softly. 'And disappointed.'

Ambiguous and contrasting feelings fought a nasty little battle in Caitlin's thoughts as she struggled to know which one to bring into the open. She had a worrying suspicion that this was all a game to him, but at the same time she couldn't suppress the disturbing lift to her thoughts that came with the realisation that perhaps he really had meant his invitation seriously.

She didn't want to admit to herself that she had been struggling with disappointment at the fact that he seemed to have given in on the subject of asking her out. That, deep inside, she had wanted him to try again, even though she had known she would give the same answer.

She didn't want to go out to dinner with him, she told herself—go anywhere with him. But all the same she didn't want to think she was so instantly forgettable.

'You really wanted to have dinner?'

'I wouldn't have asked otherwise.'

'And you said no?' Bob interrupted again. 'I think it's just what you need.'

'But if it's company policy...' Rhys inserted with just the right amount of understanding to convince her father and at the same time set her teeth on edge.

'Mr Delaney, I don't know where you've got the idea that I frown on my employees socialising with guests, but believe me, there is no such rule. And besides, this could be just what my Cait needs. She's had a hard time lately—'

'Dad, I can't!' Caitlin broke in hastily, before her father could launch into a detailed and unwelcome explanation of the disasters and the miseries of the past year. She felt vulnerable enough already without exposing this wounded part of herself to a complete stranger. 'I can't leave the baby!'

This last remark was hissed at him in what she hoped was a secret undertone. But the secret bit didn't work. The dark head of the man before her came up sharply, blue eyes swinging to her face and narrowing swiftly.

'You have a—a baby?'

Hell and damnation, Rhys cursed himself furiously. He'd very nearly messed up badly there. He'd known what she'd been about to say—the next excuse she would roll out to avoid having dinner with him. And as a result he had almost reacted in quite the wrong way.

It had taken him a couple of all too revealing seconds to realise that he should be reacting in total surprise and confusion, not with the 'Yeah, I *know* that' his thoughts were forming.

Except that Sean might have mentioned to Caitlin their conversation about the baby. Which left him totally confused about what he could or could not say.

And so when he *did* speak, rushing in to cover his momentary hesitation, he sounded as shocked and disapproving as any maiden aunt learning of the baby for the first time.

Clearly Caitlin thought so too.

'She's not mine!' she responded with sharp defensiveness. 'She's—she was—my cousin's child.'

'We've had a bereavement in the family recently,' Bob put in by way of an explanation.

'I'm sorry.'

He had to force himself to say it. Not that he wasn't sorry that Amelie was dead. She had been so vivid and bright and full of life that no one could have known her and not felt sadness that she had gone. But his wife had walked out on him, not once, but twice. Once when she had said that she never wanted children. And the second time when, after a pretence at a 'reconciliation', she'd realised he'd guessed she only wanted him for his money. He'd been used once too often to have any affection left.

Besides, it stuck in his throat to sympathise with these two, who had taken advantage of his wife's death to steal away his child and keep her for themselves.

'So you're looking after her baby?'

'That's right.'

'Doesn't she have a father?'

Father and daughter exchanged a swift, secret look of something shared. Something they were not prepared to let the world in on.

'They were badly estranged—Amelie and her husband.' It was Bob who explained. 'And he was never interested in children. In fact he told her to have an abortion—that's why they split up.'

'*What?*'

This time, Rhys just couldn't help himself. In spite of every effort he put into holding it back, the raw-voiced exclamation of shock and disbelief escaped him.

Amelie had claimed that *he'd* wanted her to have an abortion? How could she? How *dared* she?

And how dared these people…?

'I know. You can't imagine it, can you?'

For a couple of dazed seconds he couldn't even interpret Bob's tone, let alone recognise what had motivated it. But then he saw the way the older man was thinking.

He'd taken Rhys's outburst as an indication that he was appalled by Amelie's husband's behaviour. Somehow, just when he thought he had given himself away, he had apparently managed quite the opposite.

Bob Richardson was looking at him with open approval and even his daughter seemed to have eased up on her 'you are the spawn of the devil' stance. She was actually looking at him with less than total loathing in her eyes. Ruthlessly he pressed home his advantage.

'How lucky that you were there to take the—a little girl—?' this time he managed to sound more as if he was feeling his way into the subject '—take her in.'

'We couldn't do anything else.'

It was Caitlin who spoke, sounding strangely defensive, for no reason that Rhys could see. And there was a wary look about the golden eyes that piqued his curiosity sharply. She was holding something back. And every instinct he possessed told him that it was something she was holding back from her father too.

'Of course not.'

God, but he hated having to sound so soothing, so much in agreement. But it was the only way.

He suspected that if he made his move now, went in all guns blazing, he would be very much in danger of frightening her into total flight. He could push her to snatch up the baby and run—and if she did then his weeks of careful investigating would all be for nothing. It could be months before he found her again.

Months before he held his baby daughter in his arms.

The baby whose name he didn't even know yet.

So instead he swallowed down the anger and forced himself to maintain the soft-toned approach.

'We wouldn't need to go very far. We could have dinner in the hotel if that would suit.'

'Oh, that—' Belatedly Bob Richardson realised it was not up to him to answer. 'Cait?' He threw her a speaking look. 'I'll babysit for you.'

Caitlin knew what that look meant. Her father wanted her to do this. He thought it would be good for her.

And the truth was that it probably *would* be good for her. She couldn't lock herself away and mourn Josh for the rest of her life.

Perhaps she'd had it all wrong, she thought, looking into the blue, blue eyes of the man in front of her. There was nothing about this Matthew Delaney that should worry her. The problem had all been with her from the start.

'Well?'

'I—I don't know.'

'I really would like it if you'd have dinner with me,' he said softly. And at her side Caitlin felt her father stir and move away quietly and tactfully. 'Please.'

What could she say? How could she refuse when those brilliant eyes were fixed on her face, and his voice had softened so enticingly as he'd added that final word?

Admit it, a voice whispered inside her head. Go on, admit the truth. You're flattered and frankly stunned that a man as good-looking and charismatic as this should be interested in you. After Josh, and his betrayal, you find it hard to believe that anyone like this would want you to have dinner with them.

Josh had been a stunningly good-looking man, and wealthy too. She had always thought that it just wasn't possible he would choose her over anyone else. She had been convinced that one day someone more equal to him would come along and he'd lose interest and go with her instead.

And when Amelie had come into their lives, her suspicions had proved exactly right.

But was that any reason to turn down this man's invitation?

'Who left the rose?'

His response was a wide, wicked grin that lifted her heart and did disturbing things to her blood pressure, making her pulse tap-dance excitedly.

'Young Sean,' he said simply, openly. 'I think he has a terrible crush on you. But don't tell him I told you.'

'I won't…'

How could she say anything else when he was letting her off the hook in a way? He could have made a big thing of the fact that she had suspected him—accused him openly.

'And—and yes. I will have dinner with you tonight.'

If he had made any clever comment, or looked triumphant—anything that made her feel edgy in any way—then she would have changed her mind and hastily withdrawn her agreement.

But he didn't. He just smiled, briefly and gently and alarmingly pleasantly, and murmured, 'Thank you,' in a low, husky voice that made her toes curl in quick reaction.

'Would eight o'clock suit you?'

'It should be fine. I'll just check the bookings diary.'

She was glad of a chance to escape and move to the reception desk, concentrating her attention on pulling out the diary, riffling through the pages and finding the date. It was as she bent her head over it that she heard him come close up behind her.

'Eight's a problem…'

She studiously avoided looking at him, her heart jumping erratically in response to his silent closeness so that she knew her colour must be heightened, her eyes over-bright.

'But if we make it half-past?'

'That'll suit me.'

'Great.'

As she scribbled down the appointed time, a lock of soft brown hair fell forward over her face, getting into her eye. With an exclamation of annoyance she brushed it back, tucking it behind her ear.

The tiny gesture did disturbing things to Rhys's struggle for composure. Already his precarious hold on his temper had been threatened by what she had told him about the baby. The rage that had boiled up inside him at the way that he—as her cousin's estranged husband—had been painted totally black was still lurking inside, barely under control.

He could only pray that his outward appearance had hidden the way that his hands had been clenched into hard fists where they were pushed deep into his pockets.

But now another feeling clutched at his guts, twisting sharply. A different, but equally primitive feeling. A physical hunger that burned away thought.

But not all thought.

Because, totally unexpectedly, mixed in with the most basic, most primal hunger, he had a sudden rush of sympathy. Of tenderness. A longing to hold and protect—to *cherish* this woman.

It was the line of her cheek that did it. The delicate curve of her jaw, the faintly rose-tinted pallor of her skin.

They were fine and feminine and totally irresistible. And he couldn't fight the appeal they made to his senses.

His mouth felt dry, his throat tightening. He leaned closer, the faint, floral scent of her perfume swirling round him like a fragrant cloud. His thoughts swam, his body tightening, and he could barely see as his lips came closer, touched the fine-skinned area under her ear and pressed a soft, lingering kiss to the warmth of her flesh.

Caitlin froze for a second, then reacted sharply. Her head swung round, translucent eyes wide and startled.

'What—?'

Anger was the first thing that sprang to her tongue. Anger and rejection.

But as soon as her gaze locked with the deep blue of his, suddenly the rejection evaporated. And the anger vanished immediately afterwards. Instead she had the scarily composure-shaking feeling that she was looking into the eyes of fate. Of something she didn't yet understand, but which was going to affect her life forever.

'Did that break the rules?' he questioned softly. 'Because if it did then I can't say I'm sorry.'

'Yes—no…' Caitlin managed, not sure at all how she should answer or even what she was answering.

Rules? What rules? It seemed as if even ordinary, everyday life had lost its meaning and her grip on life was slipping away from her fingers.

'No,' she decided at last and that seemed to be the answer that pleased him. At least his eyes seemed less dangerous, and his mouth curved faintly at the corners into something that was almost a smile.

'I couldn't resist it. I wanted to kiss you. I have done from the start. Just as I wanted you to have dinner with me tonight.'

'I—I'm glad. I wanted it too.'

And the really scary thing, Caitlin reflected as she watched him walk away, tall, dark, devastating and totally disruptive to her peace of mind, was just how true that was.

CHAPTER THREE

'I THINK it's time we left.'

Rhys glanced briefly at his watch then lifted a hand to summon the hovering waiter.

'Do you realise that we are the only people left in here?'

'Are we?'

Startled, Caitlin glanced round her sharply, the movement reflected and repeated over and over in the dozens of gold-framed mirrors that lined the walls of the restaurant.

'Where did everyone go?'

'To the bar. To their rooms. To bed.'

Was it only in his mind that those words had the sensual echoes that reverberated around them, like the ripples from a stone thrown into the stillness of a pond? Or had the big golden eyes that had focused on him so intently all night suddenly darkened and deepened as if her thoughts were reflected there?

The three days since his arrival at the hotel might not have changed very much. But the three hours since she had joined him in the restaurant tonight had resulted in much more than he could have hoped for.

In those three hours, Caitlin Richardson seemed to have become another woman entirely. So much so that he hardly recognised her as the uptight receptionist who had greeted him on his arrival at the Linford.

The physical change had been the first, the most amazing thing. The shock had been so great that he had simply stared in disbelief, all hope of speech deserting him. And for the first time in the months since he had learned of his daughter's existence, all recollection of the baby fled from his mind in a second.

He had only one thought in his head and that was that he *wanted* this woman. He wanted her so badly that it hurt like a kick in the gut, making him fight to suppress a groan of response.

The neat navy and white uniform she had worn had been replaced by a silk dress in a deep, rich peacock-blue, tight-fitting and clinging all the way down her elegant frame to just above her knees. The bodice was sleeveless, strapless, boned in a way that enhanced the slight curves of her small breasts, lifting and displaying them in a way that made his breath catch in his throat, struggling to force his eyes away. And over it she wore a gauzy top of some toning, transparent fabric that flattered the delicate ivory of her skin, shading and defining it in a subtly enticing way. Fine shoes, so fragile as to be almost non-existent, with a small, thin heel, emphasised the slender length of her legs sheathed in the finest silken stockings.

The soft brown hair that had been so ruthlessly scraped back before now hung in a sleek and glossy mane, and the way that it caught the light from the elaborate chandelier showed that it had strands of bronze and gold gleaming amongst the brown, like the glow of the softest candlelight. And some skilful touch with make-up had made her eyes huge, her lashes thick and impossibly long, her mouth soft and glossy and tormentingly kissable.

But the biggest change had been in her personality. Just like her hair, she had softened and warmed, seeming determined to relax and enjoy herself. She had smiled. She had laughed. She had chatted easily and apparently openly. And she had given every impression of enjoying the evening thoroughly.

Which gave him hope for moving the next stage of his plan along before too long.

And added the kick of anticipated pleasure to sweeten the mixture he was aiming for.

'Would you like a drink in the bar—a liqueur, or brandy?'

'No, I think not. I'd better get back.'

Was that regret in her voice? He certainly hoped so. It sounded as though she was reluctant to leave.

Reluctance suited him down to the ground.

'I'll walk with you.'

That brought a look of surprise and frank disbelief to her face.

'I only have about a hundred yards to go.'

'But I always walk my date home at the end of the evening.'

He watched her register the word 'date', turn it over in her mind, debate with herself whether she was going to let him get away with it.

'There's no need—'

'Caitlin—' he broke in sharply '—let me do this.'

He'd pitched his voice just right—aiming at a blend of concern and insistence, with a touch of need threading through it. And he knew he'd hit home as she opened her mouth to refuse, then stilled, and carefully closed it again.

'Matthew, I really don't think this is necessary.'

'But I do.'

She couldn't know what it did to him to hear her voice, soft and faintly husky, use his name—or at least the name that he had given her. Something twisted sharply deep inside in response and he had to clamp his mouth tight shut against the sudden impulse to tell her the truth.

He would have to do so sooner or later, but first he hoped to win her round to viewing him with at least a degree of favour. That way he would have the advantage of her when he finally revealed why he was here.

When he demanded that she hand his child over to him.

But at the same time there was a need that tied his nerves into knots. The need to hear her use his real name. And to use it other than in a way to try and put him off.

He could just imagine what those soft tones would sound like in the darkness of the bedroom. In the sensual aftermath of lovemaking. In the height of passion...

Oh, hell—no!

He was intensely grateful that the need to open the heavy swing doors, to stand back, holding one while she went before him, was activity enough to distract both her attention and his from the embarrassingly frank way his body was betraying him. He was hard and hot and hungry, his pulse thudding dangerously.

The blast of cool night air in his face from the courtyard outside did something for the heat, but little to ease the hunger, or the race of his pulse. And quite frankly the sight of Caitlin's elegant form, just a couple of metres in front of him, with her straight back, slim hips, the curves of her buttocks swaying as she moved, only worsened the way he was feeling. So much so that he paused, fighting his reactions, struggling for control.

It was a long, long time since he had felt like this about any woman. And it was damned inconvenient that it should happen now, with *this* woman. When he needed to be in control of every move, every thought. When he wanted to make sure that he was the winner, not her.

'Matthew?'

She had stopped a short distance away and was looking back, a faint frown creasing the space between her brows.

'Matthew?' she said again and he realised that for a few dangerously revealing seconds he hadn't recognised his as-

sumed name and was too slow reacting to it. 'I thought you
wanted to walk me back.'

'And I got the distinct impression that you didn't want
me to bother.'

Damn. He'd aimed for sounding offhand and missed it
by a mile.

'So what is it to be, Caitlin? Yes or no?'

What is it to be? The words swirled round in Caitlin's
thoughts as she struggled to find an answer. Any answer.
An answer that would get her off this emotional see-saw
she had been riding ever since this man had appeared in
her life.

She had felt, if not happy, then at least secure. If she let
nothing new into her life, nothing emotional, then nothing
could hurt her. At least that was the way she had reasoned.
But then this Matthew had walked into the hotel and
seemed to have blasted straight through the defences she
had built around herself and her heart

He had touched her; mentally if not physically. And she
didn't want to be touched.

'Well?'

Why did she get the idea that he was asking much more
than the simple question that had started this? Looking back
at him, she could see how the moonlight had fallen on his
face so that she could see only one half of it. The profile
that was directly towards her. The rest of his features were
totally in shadow, unseen and totally impossible to interpret.

Which fitted with the way she felt about him. The idea
she had that he was not really showing her his true self.
That she could only see one part of him. The part that was
in the light.

But what about the part that was in the darkness?

No, she was being ridiculous! Determinedly she gave

herself a brisk mental shake, wanting to dispel the foolish fantasies that were clouding her thoughts. What could he do to her, for heaven's sake? What could happen in a short walk, with the lights and the windows of the hotel rooms on all sides?

And why was she saying no when the truth was that she wanted to say…?

'Yes.'

The response slipped past her lips before she had time for a second thought and when he moved to her side she knew she didn't want to think again. Once more that unexpected feeling of being young, female and *alive* bubbled up inside her and she knew she was going to go with it.

She *wanted* to go with it.

She had been alone too long. Much longer than anyone in her family realised. She had enjoyed herself tonight with this stunning, charming, fascinating man. And for the first time in long, lonely months she had forgotten that her lover—the man she had believed was a heartbeat away from becoming her fiancé—had betrayed her with her cousin Amelie.

And so when his hand bumped against hers, as so often happened when two people were walking together, she didn't snatch hers away, but let it linger suggestively.

He took the hint and folded his fingers around hers, warm and hard and strong, and the sheer reality of his touch grabbed at the breath in her throat, stilling it and holding it captive just for a second. And when she could breathe again she felt light-headed with the rush of oxygen to her brain. And the rush of something else, very different, very primitive, to other, ultra-feminine parts of her body.

'I enjoyed myself tonight,' she told him. 'The meal was wonderful.'

'You have your father's chef to thank for that.'

'For the food, yes. Marcel is brilliant. But it was the company I enjoyed more.'

'I'm glad you felt that way.' His voice was low and sounded huskily sincere. 'I enjoyed it too.'

Already they had made their way down the paved path and come to the bottom of the steps that led up to the small building that formed her home. Caitlin paused and glanced up at him.

'Well, here we are—home safe and sound, after that long, difficult journey.'

The grin that spread across his face in response to her gentle teasing was wide, brilliant and totally unrestrained. His face was in the full light of the lamp so that she could see both sides of it, bright and clear. And the formerly hidden, the shadowed side was just the same as the rest, open and friendly, and devastatingly, lethally attractive.

And what had she been expecting? she reproved herself sharply. She had to stop being so stupidly fanciful.

'You've done your duty. Brought me home.'

'Safe and sound.'

One long finger reached out to rest against her cheek, and he bent his dark head very slightly, looking deep into her eyes.

'So this is goodnight...'

'It doesn't have to be.'

She didn't know she was going to say the words until she heard them floating on the cool night air.

'You always see your dates home...I always offer mine coffee when they walk me to my door. So...'

'Yes.'

He didn't pretend to need any further explanation of what she meant. Even as he spoke his arm was coming round her shoulders, sliding down her back to her waist, turning her slightly towards the steps. And then he dropped a soft, tender kiss on her upturned face.

'And I always say yes.'

Caitlin felt as if the arm at her back had lifted her from the ground, as if her feet weren't treading on the damp stone of the steps, but she was almost floating upwards towards her door. They started slow but then the pressure at her waist increased and her movements picked up speed until she was almost running, running to the top and across the tiny courtyard.

She actually let an exclamation of annoyance and impatience escape her at the thought that the door was shut— that she would have to fumble for her key, delaying more than she wanted the time when she was alone with this man in the privacy of her home.

'At last!'

The words escaped her in an instinctive sigh and she could have sworn that she heard them echoed, an octave lower, by Matthew as he came through the door behind her, his movements hurried and abrupt as a sudden cloudburst threatened to drown him in a torrential downpour.

'I am *so* glad that you invited me in!' he declared, shaking his dark head so that raindrops flew from his hair, spattering against the walls.

'Because of the rain?' Caitlin teased, unexpectedly breathless and knowing it had nothing to do with the rush up the steps and through the door.

There was laughter in his face as he turned to look at her. But the amusement faded, ebbing away fast as his eyes met hers, locked and held.

'No, not because of the rain,' he said in a voice that was rough-edged and dark. 'Because of this...'

Reaching out, he caught hold of her arm, pulling her towards him, not roughly but not gently either. She came up against the hard strength of his body with a force that knocked some of the breath from her body. Breath that she hadn't quite been aware of holding in until she heard the faint, shocked, 'Ooof!' that escaped her.

It was the only sound she was capable of as his arms folded round her, enclosing her tightly, and his head came down, the skin of his cheek cold and fresh with the night air against her own.

But the mouth that captured hers was hot. Hot as hell— or did she mean hot as heaven?

Because heaven had to feel like this. Like this rich, violent rush of joy that almost made her swoon away from its impact on her senses. The thick, ragged pounding of her heart forcing the blood through her veins with an almost savage throb. And the instant, yearning response that met his kiss with another of her own, with a need and a hunger that was a delight in the same moment that it veered dangerously close to pain.

Heaven had to be this bright, this burning, this unbelievable.

So much so that the loss of it felt like the loss of life itself.

Because it didn't last. It couldn't last at this intensity and keep her here, upright, in the real world. As it was, her mind had stopped functioning and she felt as if the top of her head had been blown off. And the wooden floor seemed to be swaying under her feet, rocking her balance dreadfully.

'Matthew…' she choked.

Her hands went up, clutching at his shoulders, holding on tight for fear of falling.

'Mat—'

But her thoughts had been right. It couldn't last. As she tried to get his name past the tightness in her throat he suddenly pulled his mouth away, snatching in a deep, raw breath, and muttering something roughly.

'What?'

She tried to focus her eyes on his face, seeing nothing but a blur inches above her.

'What's wrong?'

'Wrong?'

It seemed to come from a throat almost as constricted as her own.

'Nothing's wrong—it's just—this can—should wait. Your father…'

'My father?'

Slowly it dawned on her what he meant.

'My father isn't here.'

'But I thought… He said…'

He had stiffened disturbingly, taking a step backwards, away from her. Her fingers loosened their hold, slid down the powerful length of his arms and rested just above his wrists.

'He said that he was babysitting. But he doesn't come here. He takes the baby to his flat in the main building. That way he can be on hand if anything happens—if there's any crisis he needs to be—'

'He's not here? The baby's not here?' He fired the questions at her like bullets.

'No. I told you.'

Had she done something wrong? What had she said that had changed his mood so completely?

'Matthew?'

Impulsively she tightened her hold on him, feeling the strength of muscle tauten and jerk under her hand.

'Don't!'

Roughly he pulled away, turned towards the door. Caitlin's heart jolted painfully in her chest in sudden fear.

Was he leaving her? About to walk out? But why? Only a moment before...

Her breathing started up again on a wave of relief as he seemed to hesitate, then, grabbing hold of the door, slammed it shut with far more force than was necessary, even allowing for the rain driving into the narrow hallway.

'So the—your father's not here. Or the baby?'

'No. I told you—they're both at the main house.'

What was putting that dark edge on his voice, making it the voice of a stranger, not the charming, flatteringly attentive man who had been her companion at dinner? The man who had poured her wine with a liberal hand, answered her questions about his life and his job easily and apparently openly. Who had laughed at her jokes, agreed with her opinions, complimented her flatteringly on her appearance.

'What—what is it?'

Slowly he turned, drawing in a deep breath as he did so, and pushing a hand roughly through his hair. But as he came to face her again she saw to her astonishment that he was smiling in a way that made a nonsense of her fears, pushed them totally aside, sending them right back to the dark, clouded corners of her brain from which she had foolishly let them creep.

'It's nothing,' he responded lightly. 'Nothing's wrong. Quite the opposite. It's just that I thought we would have company—your father and...the child. I never expected that we would be alone.'

The relief was so great that she sagged back against the wall, unable to do anything but smile in her turn. She had been so sure that he was about to go. That somehow she had made some mistake that would drive him away, out into the darkness of the night, just when she had admitted to herself how much she wanted him to stay.

'So you don't mind?'

'Why should I mind? Haven't I spent days working towards this?'

'You—you have?'

'And you haven't noticed.'

He sounded exasperated, but she was relieved to see that his mouth still smiled, in contrast to the darkness of his eyes.

'You—you want to be alone with me?'

His smile grew wider, and he shook his head as if in exasperation at her disbelief.

'You make it sound as if it is the last thing you expected. Of course I want to be alone with you.'

'But why?'

'Why?'

It was accompanied by a scathing glance from those blue eyes. A glance that told her she could not possibly be so foolish, so appallingly naïve.

'Do you really have to ask why? You know the answer to that. Why does a man want to be alone with a woman?'

Now was her chance to say he'd got it wrong. That the arrogant assumptions he was making were totally mistaken. That she had invited him in only out of politeness, nothing more.

But how could she tell him that when she knew that it would just not be true? And she would betray herself totally to him by saying so.

'Why did you invite me in?'

'For coffee?' she ventured, knowing it had not been that at all.

His laughter told her that he had caught the hint of teasing in her tone. Caught it and understood it, driving straight through the surface of her words to what she really meant underneath.

'For coffee,' he said softly, huskily, deep blue eyes burning into hers. 'Well, if you insist, we'll start with coffee. But I think we both know only too well that that's not where it will end.'

And with the memory of that kiss still burning on her lips, the sensations it had triggered off still tingling over every inch of her body, Caitlin didn't even try to consider arguing with herself, let alone with him.

CHAPTER FOUR

RHYS prowled restlessly about the small sitting room, looking for something—anything—that would give him some clue about his baby.

He had come with Caitlin tonight in the full belief that the baby would be here, in the flat. That he would see her—his daughter—for the very first time. And the realisation that that was not going to happen had hit him like a blow to his head.

For a few dangerous moments the roar of disappointment and frustration in his mind had been like an explosion inside his skull, knocking him off balance. So much off balance that he had nearly given himself away.

He had almost let rip; almost shouted at her, yelling in his pain and frustration, making it plain that he wasn't here for the reasons she had thought.

Don't call me Matthew! The words had been on the tip of his tongue and he had only managed to swallow them down with the most violent struggle, biting them off at the last minute.

The baby wasn't here. He wouldn't see his daughter tonight. And the frustration of that fact ate at his soul like a vicious cancer.

'Put some music on if you want to.'

Caitlin's voice came through to him from the tiny kitchen, where she was setting cups out on a tray, filling a jug with milk.

'There are some CDs over in the corner. Choose whatever you like.'

'I'm fine, thanks.'

It was a struggle to make it sound even remotely believable. 'Fine' didn't just fail to describe the way he was feeling. He was a million miles away from 'fine' and the snarl of discontent in his voice revealed that only too plainly.

Or perhaps it didn't. Certainly Caitlin didn't appear to notice. But then perhaps his tone was muffled by the half-open door between them, the sound of the kettle beginning to boil.

All the same, he made himself go and study the rack of discs in the far corner of the room. Anything to reduce the chance of her feeling suspicious. To keep her from wondering if he had ulterior motives for being here.

'Anything you fancy?'

If she answered, he didn't hear. His attention was once more back on the small room he stood in. It was... He hunted for the right word.

Unrevealing.

It was the only one that fitted. The room told him little about the woman who lived in it except that she liked—he glanced down at the plastic-covered discs in his hands—folk music and classical.

The room was comfortable enough, with dove-grey armchairs and a small settee, brightened by scattered cushions in candy-coloured stripes, a huge bunch of white chrysanthemums in a green vase by the window. It was a feminine room, cool and relaxed and inviting, but had few personal touches that revealed the character of its owner. And, infuriatingly, there were no photographs. Particularly no photographs of the one tiny person he most wanted to see.

'Did you say you'd not lived here long?'

He was sorting through the discs as he spoke, shifting cases from one hand to the other, but not really seeing what was in them.

'That's right. I was working in France until…'

The clatter of cups on the tray hid whatever she had said from him.

'Then when Dad offered me the job as receptionist I came back here.'

'Bringing your cousin's baby with you?'

'Amelie wasn't really my cousin…'

The kettle whistled and Rhys heard her snatch it up from the stove, pouring the water over coffee grounds in the glass cafetière.

'My mother and hers were the real cousins—but I forget what that made us. I usually just refer to her as my cousin because it makes explanations simpler. Did you want sugar?'

'No, thanks.'

Realising that he had been staring unseeingly at the compact discs for the past minute, Rhys hurriedly dumped them back down on the shelf. Stacked precariously, the small bundle wobbled dangerously and the top disc overbalanced and slid off, crashing down to the floor.

With a muttered curse, Rhys bent to pick it up, then froze, blue eyes fixed on a tiny scrap of white that lay on the soft grey carpet, half hidden under the flounced cover of one armchair.

His mouth went dry, his throat seeming to close up. His heart lurched, thudding hard against his chest, and his eyes stung with the pressure of tears forcing themselves underneath his lids.

A bootee. A small, finely knitted bootee in soft white wool.

A baby's bootee.

He reached out to pick it up. Only to find that his hand was shaking so badly that he couldn't grip it. His vision had blurred too.

'Stop it!' he muttered to himself with fierce reproach. 'Stop it!'

On the second attempt he picked up the small object, grasping it in his hand and lifting it towards his face.

A baby's bootee.

His baby's bootee.

His daughter's...

This microscopic item he held in his hand, the wool slightly grubby and in need of a wash, was the first real, genuine evidence of his daughter's existence.

His fingers closed over it, clenching tightly, and he had the sudden, desperate feeling that he could never, ever let go. This was the first, the only time since he had discovered that she existed that he had actually touched something that had also touched his daughter's skin.

Unable to resist the impulse, he lifted the bootee to his nose and inhaled. Did it hold a lingering trace of the little person who had worn it? Was he imagining it?

'Matthew?'

Caitlin's questioning, faintly uncertain voice jarred him back to the present, to see her standing in the doorway, the tray in her hand.

'What have you found?'

'Just something that was on the floor.'

He gestured with the hand that held the bootee.

'Oh, so that's where that went! I've been hunting for it.'

'Here, let me help you with that...'

Deliberately aiming to distract her, Rhys moved forward to take the tray from her hands, hurriedly pushing the bootee into his trouser pocket as he did so. It looked as if he was just freeing his hands to help, but right now he knew that he would kill anyone who tried to separate him from that one small item.

'You sit down...'

In the flurry of getting Caitlin seated, pouring milk into his coffee, stirring it, he hoped that the revealing action had gone unnoticed. Or that if she had seen it she would soon get diverted and forget all about it.

'Were you and this Amelie close?'

He knew the answer already and could only be thankful that they hadn't been good friends. If they had, she might have been at his wedding to her cousin and then his cover would have been blown.

'Not at all. I didn't really know her very well until we met up again in France. The last time we'd seen each other had been well over ten years ago. I was twelve and she was fifteen. A very sophisticated, grown-up fifteen. She regarded me as little more than a child and looked down on me as a result.'

'So why did she ask you to look after her baby?'

'Why?'

Caitlin flinched inwardly as he put his finger unknowingly right on the spot that hurt most. For a moment she almost felt tempted to open up, tell him the truth, but just as hastily rethought. She didn't want this stunning, sophisticated, handsome man to know how badly she had been fooled, how easily deceived, and by her own cousin and her fiancé.

'I don't think she had anyone else. Her parents were both dead, and she had no brothers or sisters.'

'And the father? You didn't think to get in touch with the husband?'

The look she threw him over her coffee-cup said all that needed saying without any need for words.

'You know what I think about him.'

'How do you know your cousin was telling the truth?'

It was sharp, unexpectedly hard, like the probing questioning of counsel for the prosecution, and it made Caitlin shift nervously where she sat.

'She wouldn't have lied to me. And besides, it's nothing to do with him.'

It was nothing to do with him because Amelie's husband, Rhys, had no claim at all. He wasn't the baby's father. Not according to Josh.

'I promised Amelie I'd care for her child. That was all that was important.'

'So when are you going to fetch her back here?'

'I'm not—she's staying with Dad tonight.'

'All night?'

The blue eyes looked startled, almost shocked.

'Will he know what to do?'

'He's done it before.'

He still looked sceptical, the indigo eyes narrowed in concentrated assessment.

'She'll be fine!'

She frowned her puzzlement, seeing him with new and very different eyes.

'You surprise me. Most men wouldn't even be interested.'

'I'm not most men! Some of us are interested—more than interested. Some men care about children, perhaps even more than some women! You've said it's nothing to do with your cousin's husband—but what if he doesn't think that way? What if he *wants* to look after his child?'

The bite in his voice slashed at her, leaving her feeling uneasy. She didn't know quite where she had overstepped some line that she hadn't even been aware of him having laid down, but it worried her. She just wanted to go back, retrace their conversational footsteps to a point where they were relaxed together again.

'I—I know that. Why do you think I told you about my

cousin in the first place? I have to be pretty wary. I mean, I know that Amelie told me her husband didn't want children—but I've always been scared that he might just turn up. Demand that I hand her over.'

'Ah, so that's it? That's why you reacted to the suggestion of a simple date as if I'd asked you to sell your soul.'

Embarrassed colour washed Caitlin's face. Leaning forward to put her cup down on the coffee-table, she twisted in her seat so that she was facing him, one leg curled up under her on the settee.

'I think I owe you an apology.'

He swallowed down his coffee in something of a rush and once more studied her intently over the top of his cup.

'You do?'

Caitlin nodded firmly, sending her hair flying so that it distracted him, his dark blue gaze following the movement. With nervous fingers she smoothed it behind her ears once again and switched on a flashing smile.

'When you first arrived, I wasn't exactly polite. It's just I was thrown off balance. I—I haven't been asked out for a long time.'

This time the look he slanted at her from beneath thick black lashes was one of frank disbelief.

'You don't have to fish for compliments...'

'I'm not! I mean—that isn't what I meant. People don't ask you out when you're in a long-term relationship.'

'You have someone in your life?'

Caitlin thought of the space that Josh had left in her life. A space that his daughter now filled for her.

'Very much so.'

'I see.'

She couldn't mistake the message in the way that Rhys stiffened, moved away slightly, setting down his half-drunk

coffee with the obvious intention of getting to his feet—
and walking right out the door.

'I don't get involved with anyone already in a relationship—there are too many complications there.'

'No!'

Impulsively Caitlin reached out, caught hold of his arm
to still him when he would have got to his feet.

'I mean we *were* together—once. We're not now.'

For a second he tensed as if about to shake her hand off,
then he subsided back down amongst the cushions.

'Go on,' he said, though his tone had nothing encour-
aging in it.

'He—he met someone else. In fact he was seeing her—
sleeping with her—while we were still together.'

She stumbled over the words, the bitterness burning on
her tongue, making it almost impossible to force the words
out. She didn't want to remember. But she had to explain.

'He—was unfaithful to me for months before I even suspected.'

'I see.'

It was cold, flat, unemotional.

'And your fiancé…'

'Joshua…'

'This Joshua—is he with this woman now?'

'Oh, yes…'

Cruel tears pushed at the backs of Caitlin's eyes but she
refused to let them fall. Joshua and Amelie had died in the
same accident. They couldn't be much more *together* than
that.

'Yes. He's very much with her now.'

'But he's still a part of your life.'

It was only when the man beside her drew in a deep
breath and pushed both his hands through the gleaming
darkness of his hair that she realised how she had been

staring into the distance, her unfocused eyes seeing nothing, trapped in the bitterness of her memories. His sudden movement made her jump slightly, turning her wide, startled gaze on his shuttered face.

'It's a permanent thing,' she managed with brittle cynicism.

But he wasn't listening.

'Caitlin,' he said, something dark and secret roughening his tone, 'there are some things I have to tell you. We have to talk.'

'No!'

It spilled from her instinctively, without a hope of being held back. It was an instant, uncontrollable impulse, created by the pain of the memories she wanted to forget.

'No talking.'

Josh had said, 'We have to talk.' It was the way he had prefaced telling her the truth.

We have to talk, he had said, but the fact was that Caitlin had hardly said a word. She had been too shocked, too devastated to open her mouth. And her tongue seemed to have frozen solid, incapable of movement.

'Josh said we had to talk—and he *talked* all right! Oh, yes, he poured it all out—didn't seem able to stop. How he had never meant to hurt me, but he hadn't been able to help himself. How he'd just seen her and fallen head over heels—how he wanted to be with her...'

She broke off abruptly as Rhys leaned forward, putting one hand over hers to stop the bitter flow of her words.

'That's talking,' he said quietly.

'So it is.'

Her mouth twisted into a wry grimace.

'I'm sorry.'

'Do you want to tell me about it?'

'I think I've already said more than enough.'

It was sharp, vehement, emphatic. She didn't want to revive those memories; didn't want to recall them at all. For the first time she had put them behind her, out of her mind, and she wanted them to stay that way.

'So what do you want to do?'

She looked up into his darkly watchful face. She had been studying that face throughout the evening, opposite her, across the table, in the candlelight. The blue eyes, the long, thick lashes, the sensual mouth…

She'd watched that mouth with a fierce concentration. She'd seen it smile, laugh, sometimes twist cynically. She'd seen him touch his napkin to it, raise his glass, and when it came away the firm fullness of his lips had been stained faintly with the rich burgundy of the wine.

And it had been impossible not to wonder—to imagine the feel of it on her mouth, on her skin…

'Caitlin?'

'I want you to kiss me.'

It clearly wasn't the last thing he was expecting. His reaction showed no surprise, no hint of shock. Instead he just inclined his head slightly, those deep blue eyes widening, darkening, and the sensual mouth that had so fascinated her curled into the faintest hint of a smile.

Leaning forward, he touched his lips to her cheek, soft and warm and enticing.

'Like this?'

Sanity begged her to say yes. To say that was what she had wanted. All she had wanted.

That was the safe way.

But safety wasn't what she wanted. She had thought that she was safe with Josh and their future, but it had only taken a day or two to turn that on its head and leave her, even though she hadn't known it at the time, standing with the ruins of what she had thought her life to be lying all around her.

She'd had enough of safety. She didn't believe in it any more.

'No.'

It was a moan of protest, of complaint.

'No, that's not what I want. Not enough.'

She heard his breath draw in between his teeth, met the deep intensity of his gaze head on and read her fate in it.

'Then tell me what you want, Caitlin. Show me.'

It took the space of a heartbeat, the tiniest of movements, to turn her head until her mouth met his, until their lips were against each other, their breath mingling, their eyes locked.

'I want this…' she said and took his mouth in a slow, lingering kiss. 'I want this—and more.'

His only audible response was faintly muffled laughter, but his physical response was all she had wanted. His lips took the kiss from her and returned it with full force. Slow and sensual and growing in demand with each second that ticked by. His tongue slid out and ran along the opening of her mouth, promising, enticing, provoking.

And Caitlin gave herself up to that provocation.

Her mouth opened to him, a faint sigh of surrender escaping, turning into a sound of pure longing and need. And, hearing it, he reached out, enfolded her in his arms, holding her hard against him. A slight twist of his body, a hint of pressure on hers, brought her down onto the back of the settee, her hair supported by the soft grey cushions, her face lifted up to receive the force of his mouth.

For long, heated, mind-swirling seconds she was lost in sensation. In the taste of him on her tongue, the warmth of his body surrounding her, the scent of his skin against her own. And the heavy, yearning thud of her heart made her blood pound inside her skull in some ancient, primitive rhythm of need, the steady march of hungry senses along the heated path that could only lead to one inevitable end.

'Then we're thinking alike,' he murmured, his voice raw and thick and echoing the need that was building up inside her. 'We both want the same thing.'

Wanted it enough to discard the warning shouts of his beleaguered brain, Rhys acknowledged inwardly. He had fought that battle long enough and quite frankly he was tired of it. The baby wasn't here, wouldn't be here tonight. Tomorrow he would see her, hold her...

He had concentrated on that hunger for so long that he felt he had been almost erased in the process. Tonight he had other hungers, other needs. Ones that this woman could share with him. He could feel the wanting in her restless body as she stirred against him, making him harden and ache in cruel demand. And one by one his thinking processes shut down.

The delicate, transparent top she wore over the elegant dress almost melted away under the pressure of his hands, discarded somewhere on the settee beside them. Her skin felt like warm silk under his touch, soft and fine and delicately perfumed. He bent his head to kiss all the way up one arm, and across the smooth curve of a shoulder, and felt her heart kick hard as his lips touched the pulse point at the base of her neck.

'Matt...' she sighed longingly. 'Matt...'

The single syllable of the assumed name, the *wrong* name, sounded foreign and disturbingly alien in his ears, shaking him out of the sensual haze he was in. He wanted to deny it, to reject it—to refuse even to allow her to use it.

'No!'

It was harsh and rough, a jarring sound of rejection, and

it forced open those stunning golden eyes, so that they looked into his in sharp concern.

'No?' she questioned in obvious uncertainty.

It was like receiving a dash of cold water in his face. Like the unwanted invasion of chill reality into the heated haven they had created for themselves.

He could tell her, he thought. And if he told her then he knew what would happen. She would be gone before he had finished speaking. She would be away and off this sofa—out of the room before he had a chance to stop her.

'What is it?'

Rhys shook his head to collect his wandering thoughts. Was he seriously thinking of telling her who he was and why he was here? Telling *her*—this woman who hadn't even let him know that his wife was dead, that his child had been born?

Was he seriously concerned about keeping the truth from her when she had so ruthlessly kept an even greater one from him?

'What *is* it?' It was sharper now, more edgily anxious. 'What's wrong?'

Suddenly it was as if something had dawned on her and she dragged her mouth from his, leaning back so that she could look up into his face, amber eyes travelling over every inch of his features in deep concern.

'Are you—are you married?'

The relief at the fact that her question was so easy to answer had him throwing his head back and actually laughing out loud.

'Is that what you thought? Isn't it a little too late to concern yourself with that now?'

But laughter had been the wrong response, putting a new tension into her slender frame, an uneasy, anxious light into her eyes.

'Answer the question! Yes or no. Are you married?'

'No.'

He met her burning gaze head-on as he answered, his voice deep and firm, totally unwavering.

'No, I can assure you that I am not married. I was—but not any more. I have no wife. There is no other woman— *no one*—who can come between you and me.'

At least not tonight, he told himself as her eyes closed briefly and a smile of relief crept over her mouth. There was no one who could come between them tonight.

'So why the no?'

Somehow he managed to force his mouth into a lazy smile that hid his real feelings.

'You don't think I meant no, I don't want this, do you? What I was trying to say is don't let's rush this—let's take our time. And let's do things properly—I want you in a bed with me, not some frantic fumble on an uncomfortable sofa.'

The explanation reassured her, he saw as the smile grew and the light came back on in her eyes. She had no more questions in her mind—for tonight.

Tomorrow, when he told her who he was and demanded access to his daughter, it would be so very different.

But tonight was tonight, he acknowledged as he kissed her lips once more and felt her immediate, unhesitating response, the way she pressed against him, the shuddering pleasure that rippled through her body.

Tonight was theirs.

And tomorrow could take care of itself.

CHAPTER FIVE

'I REALLY think we'd be more comfortable somewhere else.'

At first Caitlin only heard the sound of the words, not registering their meaning. She was too far gone in the burn of sexuality. Too adrift in feeling to allow any other sense like hearing to function properly.

'Caitlin?'

Yes. Whatever you want. Wherever you want.

It was what she wanted to say but her voice wouldn't work either. She could barely open her eyes. The lids felt heavy and would only lift far enough to leave a slit through which she could make out the blur that was his face.

He had kissed her senseless. Caressed every inch of her exposed skin until she felt that her flesh was throbbing with need, and she couldn't focus her thoughts on anything beyond the feel and taste and scent of him. She was drugged on his touch and his kisses.

And the heat and hunger that pulsed between her thighs.

'Caitlin!'

His voice was sharper now, taut with reproof. And with something else, something that echoed the yearning hunger deep inside her.

'I'm perfectly happy to make love to you right here if that's the way you want it,' he muttered in a tone that was rough with impatience. 'But as I said, this settee is just a little cramped and I really think that the comfort of a bed...'

'Upstairs...'

Somehow she managed to form the word this time, hating the way she had to drag her mouth from his for the few seconds it took to frame it. She wanted him so much. Every bit of him. Every touch, every taste, every scent…

'Let's go upstairs.'

He let her roll out from under him on the small settee, then slither to the floor. But she barely had time to land before he caught her arms and pulled her upright, his lips fastening on hers with renewed demand.

'Upstairs,' he echoed thickly. 'Show me where.'

Caitlin was never quite sure how they made it out of the sitting room and into the hall. They were both walking blind, their eyes fixed on the other's face, their lips still kissing, tasting, nipping at each other's mouth. And yet somehow they reached the foot of the stairs, but no further. Instead he slammed her back against the wall and kissed her hard and hot, his mouth yearning, his breathing ragged.

'Do you know what you do to me?' he demanded. 'How you make me feel? How much I want you?'

'I think I can guess,' she teased and moved with deliberately wicked provocation, rubbing the cradle of her pelvis softly on the heated hardness of his forceful erection.

'Caitlin!'

Her name was a choking sound in his throat.

'Do you want me to throw you on the floor and take you here and now? Because that's what you're risking if you don't stop tormenting me.'

The way she was feeling she didn't think she'd mind. She didn't even think she'd have the strength to protest if he tried it. But still she couldn't resist teasing him just a little bit more.

'You're the one who insisted on a bed,' she whispered against his ear, letting the warm tip of her tongue trace the curving line of its outer edge, the softness of his lobe.

Her smile grew wide as she heard his groan of sensual near-agony.

'And I'm taking you upstairs to find you one.'

'I don't think I'll make it.'

'I'll make it worth your while.'

She was moving as she spoke, sliding towards the first step, inching upwards so that he was forced to come with her or lose the burning contact that made her feel as if her body was melting into his.

'I promise you a kiss for every step…'

She gave him the caress he had earned by managing to come up alongside her now.

'There are only twelve of them. Surely you can manage that.'

His only response was another groan, making the laughter bubble in her throat.

'Just twelve—eleven now…'

She slid up to the next level, her back against the wall, her breasts and hips brushing sinuously against him as she moved.

'And ten…'

The number was crushed against her lips as he moved with unexpected swiftness, coming up beside her and taking the kiss she had promised.

This time she was the one who almost weakened. The one whose body sagged, whose knees nearly gave way. But he was there, so close that she could wind her arms around his neck, let her weight rest on his shoulders as somehow she managed to find the strength to climb once more.

'Nine…' He took the number from her.

It was whispered against her breasts, deliberately provoking, his mouth hot on the exposed flesh that curved above the low neckline of her dress, his breath whispering down inside her cleavage, curling round the hardened nipples that thrust demandingly against the rich dark fabric.

'N-nine,' she echoed on a broken sigh, her heart clenching just to *imagine* what it would feel like to have his hands where his breath had been.

His mouth.

Nine steps to go. She might just make it if they hurried. She might just last the length of time it took to reach the landing, her bedroom, without going completely mad with desire. Without screaming at him to stop delaying, to stop playing with her, and take her *now*.

But no one had said that she couldn't join in the fun.

And so she bent down and pressed her own kiss on his warm and ready mouth. At the same time she stroked her fingers through his hair, slid them down over the width of his shoulders, under the edge of his collar. She felt the beat of his pulse, the warmth of his skin, and her own heart raced in reaction. Lingering deliberately, she trailed her fingers along the strong line of his throat to where his tie was tugged loose at the neck of his shirt.

'This will need to go,' she muttered, easing the button from its fastening, slipping her fingers in even further. 'And this…'

'Caitlin…'

She didn't know if his rough-voiced use of her name was protest or encouragement but she really didn't care. With the top two buttons undone, she trailed her fingers down the hard plane of his chest, swirled them round in the crisp hair that her touch encountered, then let them move lower.

'Caitlin!'

She wasn't quite aware of how he moved, how fast, how suddenly. She only knew that somehow he was beside her, his arms coming round her, swinging her up and into his grasp. There was a dangerously worrying moment when he swayed slightly and she feared that he might drop her, or fall, but it only lasted the space of an anxious heartbeat. The next second she was held firmly against him, the tensile-steel strength of his muscles supporting her easily. He looked down into her upturned face, blue, blue eyes glinting wickedly, and he grinned in fiendish triumph.

'Eight,' he said, moving on to the next step with a determined stride and then up again. 'Seven. Six—five...'

With each count his steps grew faster, more resolute, taking her upwards, swift and sure, not a second's hesitation.

'Three, two, one...'

He reached the landing, paused, looked around him only briefly, and then moved with unerring accuracy in the direction of her room.

The door was kicked open wide, and he carried her inside, only pausing when the darkness of the room, no light coming through the tightly drawn curtains, forced him to a halt.

'None,' he muttered, raw and final, and, turning her in his grasp, he lowered her slowly to the floor, letting her slide all the way down the length of his lean body, in an obviously deliberate mirroring of her teasing provocation at the bottom of the stairs.

'That's seven kisses you owe me, sweetheart,' he reminded her, holding her tight when she would have slipped away. 'You promised.'

'Only on each step!' she laughed, shaking her head in the darkness. 'That was the arrangement.'

'To hell with the arrangement!' His voice was a deep, husky growl. 'Seven kisses I'm owed, and seven kisses I'll take.'

'You haven't earned them!'

But she gave him them all the same, as she had known

she would. At least she tried. She started with one kiss, a brief, light, flirtatious caress on his demanding mouth, then dodged away again, meaning to move on to another, similar one almost at once. But two things stopped her.

The man she was kissing and her own powerful sensual hunger.

She kissed him again—and this time she couldn't get away. Her lips touched his, tasted, lingered, clung. And at the same time his hands came up around her neck, long fingers lacing in the fall of hair, curving against the bones of her skull, holding her unable to move.

And he kissed her thoroughly, hotly, hungrily. Kissed her until her head was swimming crazily and her knees threatened to buckle beneath her.

It was only when they were forced to break apart by the need to snatch in air that Rhys released her. Just enough to move her head back in order to breathe, but no more.

'Now, that's a kiss,' he told her, the air rasping into his starved lungs. 'Not the silly, half-hearted things you've been offering. A proper kiss.'

Caitlin nodded silently, struggling to breathe properly herself.

'And you owe me six more of those.'

He thought she would fight him, protest at least, but instead she swayed slightly towards him as if yearning to be closer. The faint waft of some warm, richly floral scent combined with the private aroma of her skin tormented his senses cruelly. He wanted to snatch her up again, take her in his arms and carry her to the bed, flinging her down and ripping the clinging dress from her.

He wanted to have her *now*. To bury himself in her welcoming body, sate himself with her, exhaust himself... That way, he might also drive out the unexpected and unwanted sexual pull she had for him. He had never anticipated wanting this woman so much when what he had come for was the opposite of sensual. He thought he had come for revenge. To be avenged on her for the way that she had taken his child, and kept her from him. He had thought that he could take that revenge and walk away.

Instead he found that he was obsessed by her, entangled in the sexual web she had woven around him. And he could not free himself until he knew if she could deliver what she seemed to promise. Until he had possessed her totally, steeped himself in the sensual delights her body offered.

But the tiniest lingering vestiges of common sense told him that he should take this more slowly, seduce rather than take her. He wanted her totally *his* in every way possible. Only then would she be unable to resist him, both physically and mentally.

'Is there a light in this room?' he asked, punctuating the words with a drift of kisses over her face, invisible in the darkness. 'I can't see a damn thing.'

Not that he was complaining. Not really. The blindness brought by the lack of light only served to heighten every other one of his senses, making them sharper, much more forceful, powerfully concentrated. Unable to see, he could taste and feel and smell this woman with an intensity that threatened to blow his mind, shatter his composure into a million tiny pieces.

But at the same time he knew that he wanted, needed desperately to *see* her. The moment of possession couldn't come in the darkness, blind and invisible. He wanted to look into her face in the moment that he took possession of her body, see the expression that her passion put there, the glaze of desire in her eyes. And he wanted to see how that expression changed when she climaxed, how she came apart, finally and completely in his arms, in the moment when she could hide absolutely nothing from him.

'Do we have to…?' Caitlin sounded edgy.

'Yes. I need to see you.'

With a small sound like a gulp in her throat, she moved, twisting in his arms, reaching out to some switch she could find in the dark. There was a faint click and a soft glow illuminated the room, coming from a lamp on a bedside cabinet.

'That's better. Now…'

The words faded from his tongue as he saw what else stood on the cabinet, beside the cream-shaded lamp.

The photograph in a pine-coloured frame. A photograph of a man. A tall, brown-haired, well-built man, smiling into the camera.

Or, rather, smiling at the woman behind the camera.

'Who is that?' he demanded, though he already knew the answer.

The way she hesitated, her eyes lowered, shifting awkwardly from one bare foot to another, only confirmed as much.

'Who?' Harder. Harsher. So much so that she flinched visibly.

'It's J-Josh,' she faltered clumsily.

'Josh. It's *him*, isn't it? The guy—the bastard who cheated on you.'

'Yes.'

It was little more than a whisper and she was biting down hard on her lower lip, white teeth digging into the soft fullness.

'And you keep his photo here—by your bed? Wasn't it bad enough that he messed you about that way? Do you want to be *reminded* of it?'

'I—loved him.'

'But he clearly didn't love you.'

He hated himself for saying it when he saw how she

flinched at his words. But he couldn't wish them back. How could she move on when every time she came to bed the image of this Josh was there, the last thing she saw before she fell asleep at night?

'This has to go.'

'I…'

Anger flared, hot and unthinking, when he saw how she hesitated; the way her gaze went to the frame and the face in it. Were those tears in her eyes? Did she still have feelings for the rat?

Snatching up the picture, he threw it onto the floor, bringing down his foot, heel first, on top of it, smashing the frame and the picture beneath. Shards of glass splintered round the fine black leather of his shoe, scattering like tiny diamond raindrops over the creamy-coloured carpet. Caitlin's eyes followed his actions, but she stayed silent, not even opening her mouth to protest.

'It's you and me now,' he told her harshly, his voice roughening as if it was coming from a painfully dry throat. 'And I'll not have anyone else intruding on us—least of all another man. Is that understood?'

Caitlin nodded silently, automatically, unable to do anything else. She was still staring at the mess on the floor; the shattered glass spread far and wide, the photograph of Josh's face crushed irreparably beneath his heel. And she was waiting for the pain to start.

Surely there should be some pain? Something to remind her that Josh had once been all her world, to tell her that he had carelessly broken her heart and walked away without a backward glance?

But the startling, the unbelievable thing was that she felt *nothing*. She didn't care that the frame had been destroyed; that the photograph was beyond repair. She couldn't even remember what the picture looked like under the firm, crushing pressure of this man's heel; couldn't begin to imagine Josh's once loved face in her mind.

'Caitlin?' he prompted roughly when she didn't speak. And she lifted her head, meeting the burn of those sapphire eyes head-on without hesitation.

'You and me,' she echoed steadily, unemotionally.

And it sounded wonderful. It felt amazing just to say it. It was as if a door had suddenly closed on the past and a new one had opened, wide and welcoming, drawing her onwards.

With her eyes locked with his, she took a step forwards, and then another, then paused, frowning as his hand came out to halt her.

'Careful!' he warned, and the movement of his eyes drew hers down to see how the glistening shards of glass lay on the floor around him, threatening her vulnerable, soft bare feet.

The next moment he had come towards her, reaching for her and swinging her up into his arms. A couple of swift, long strides took him out of the danger zone and to the opposite side of the bed. As he lowered Caitlin to her feet once more he kissed her long and hard, wiping the brief interlude from her mind and setting her heart beating in a very different way in a split-second.

'Now, where were we?' he murmured against her lips. 'Ah, yes—those kisses you owe me…I'll take them now.'

Caitlin was already losing her grip on reality after the first potent caress of his mouth. By the end of the second one, longer, harder, hungrily demanding, she felt as if the floor was tilting underneath her feet, forcing her to grab at the broad strength of his shoulder and hold on tight.

The third kiss was different again. Soft and slow and infinitely seductive, it beguiled her lips open, touched tongue to tongue in delicate enticement, made her want to weep for the delight of it, then reduced her to tears, of loss this time, as he gently lifted his head.

'You and me,' he said, low and deep and huskily intent.

'You—you and me,' she echoed, her control of her voice wavering as she felt his fingers on the back of her neck unclasping the long zip of her dress and sliding it all the way along her spine. The peacock-blue silk slithered down her body, pooling softly around her feet. Beneath it she wore nothing more than the laciest strips of underwear in the same rich colour, tiny suspenders holding up cobweb-fine stockings.

'Deliberate provocation...'

A strong male finger traced the fine line of skin around the top of one stocking to emphasise what he meant, and Caitlin writhed in sensual response to the heat of his touch on her flesh.

'Do I get to take them off?' His voice was pure seduction, rich warm honey flowing smoothly over polished gravel.

'Only if you lose a few clothes first,' she whispered. 'You're wearing far too many.'

'I am,' he agreed on a note of shaky laughter. 'So would you like to help me with that?'

She was already busy doing so. The touch of his hand on her leg had set her body on fire, yearning hungrily for more. She wanted, *needed* to feel him properly, know the heated sensation of skin on skin, the slide of satin over satin, the contrast of his dark, crisp body hair with the smoothness of her own limbs.

She tugged at the buttons on his shirt, opening them with more urgency than finesse, pulling his tie loose and away with her other hand. With a low, rough sound in his throat, Rhys helped her, shrugging himself out of shirt and jacket at the same time, not heeding where they fell on the floor.

It seemed to take only moments, but they were some of the longest seconds she had endured, before he was as close to naked as she was, and he tumbled with her down onto the peach-coloured cover on the bed.

'This will have to go...' he muttered, unfastening the strapless turquoise bra with a speed and skill that spoke of much practice and tossing it away to one side.

His hands took the place of the delicate lace, hard fingers hot against her yearning flesh, and immediately the atmosphere changed, tightened, becoming electrically charged with a new and urgent tension. He lifted her breasts to his mouth, kissed the rich curves, ran his tongue in erotic circles around the pouting nipples, making her catch her breath and writhe in hungry response.

'Caitlin...'

The murmur of her name against her skin was even further sensual torment that had her clutching at the crisp darkness of his hair as she strained against him.

'That feels—it feels...'

She struggled for words to describe the sensation of his lips tugging at her nipple, but abandoned the attempt on a choking cry of abandoned delight that did the job much better. A second later any hope of thought had left her as he kissed his way downwards, over the softness of her stomach, his fingers busy with the final slip of silk that kept her most feminine centre from his touch.

'That is— Oh!'

Now she could only lie back, her body tensed in concentrated delight, focusing totally on the touch of his knowing fingers on the most sensitive spot of all, driving her higher and higher, almost to the point of losing all control. But then, just as she thought she would splinter into ecstasy under his touch, he eased away, kissing a path back up her trembling body to smile down into her face.

'Ready?' he questioned huskily.

Could he doubt it? Did he have to ask? She couldn't find the words to answer him. But it seemed that after all he hadn't needed them because even as she tried to nod he raised himself slightly, pushing her legs open wider with the pressure of his own powerful thighs, and thrust himself into her in one hard, powerful movement.

'Yes,' he added on a note of slightly shaken laughter. 'Oh, yes, you were ready.'

Caitlin's eyes seemed to be losing focus. Looking up into his face, she could see only the darkness of his eyes in the shadowed room, the flare of colour marking the high, carved cheekbones, the wicked curve to his mouth as he began to move. Instantly her whole body responded, bursting into flame again, soaring, burning, reaching…reaching…

'Oh!' The choking sound of stunned surrender was pushed from her lips by wave after wave of pure amazement that something could feel this good, this fast.

'Oh—oh, Ma—'

His impatient, almost cruel mouth cut off her use of his name, stopping her breath too as he crushed her lips under his. But even as he stopped the words, his body pounded into hers, taking her out of any degree of control and over, over into a world where no thought was possible and the feeling of shattering into pieces was all she knew.

With a wild cry deep into his controlling mouth she clenched her hands hard over the strength of his shoulders, nails digging wildly into the powerfully bunched muscles, and lost herself in his embrace.

It was the start of a long, almost sleepless night.

In the heated darkness of Caitlin's bed they came together again and again, unable to have enough of each other. Each time their bodies reached new and higher levels of release, the satisfaction only seemed to serve to waken a further hunger that had them reaching for each other when their breathing had not fully had time to ease, the sheen of sweat barely dry on their skin. And each time they lost themselves in each other, only to know when thought resurfaced that they had only eased and not assuaged the stinging hunger that held them in its unrelenting grip.

The coming of the dawn had them finally tumbling into the heavy, numbing sleep of satiated exhaustion, not waking for hours until a loud, persistent noise from somewhere on the floor finally penetrated Rhys's stupor, forcing him to groan and stir.

'What the…?'

Very slowly, thought came back to him. And with thought came the recognition of the sound.

His mobile phone. Lying somewhere in a pocket of his jacket. The jacket he had discarded on the floor in such haste the previous night.

'Go away!'

He tried to close his eyes, tried to recapture the welcome oblivion of the sleep from which he was being so rudely dragged, but failed miserably. The impatient summons went on and on, refusing to be ignored.

And when, at his side, the sleeping woman who lay curved against him, her skin soft and warm against his, began to stir he knew he had to act. Another minute and the sound would waken her. And he knew that if he felt shattered after the firestorm of emotions and physical exertion that had assailed them in the night, she must be totally worn out.

She wouldn't thank him for being disturbed.

'Oh, all right!'

Leaning out of bed, he could just reach the jacket, just

snag it up and bring it within reach. Fumbling in a pocket, he reached the phone, pulled it out…

Only to have it lapse into total silence as soon as he had it securely.

'Hell and damnation!'

Letting the jacket go again, he dropped his head back onto the softness of the pillows and closed his eyes wearily, the phone still in his hand.

Just as well they'd given up, really. He didn't feel in the least like talking to anyone right now. His brain was still pleasantly scrambled from the mind-blowing sensations he had experienced, his thoughts impossible to put in order.

The only thing he could think of was Caitlin—Caitlin and her long, silky hair, her peach-soft skin. The woman with eyes like those of a wild lioness and a kiss like drug-laced honey. The woman who had taken his body and his soul and…

The shriek of the phone in his hand slashed through the sensual reverie, making him curse swiftly and savagely.

Pressing the answer button with the automatic reaction of long experience, still with his eyes half-shut, he lifted the phone to his ear.

'Rhys Morgan,' he said impatiently, the clinging shreds of sleep still slurring his words. 'Yes?'

It was Sarah Nicolaides, his invaluable personal assistant who was also a friend. Sarah, who, although now two months pregnant with her first child, had agreed to take charge of the gallery for him until he found his daughter and brought her back to London with him.

The only person he would trust to do that. And the only person he would find himself able to speak to now without blasting their head off in anger at being disturbed.

So he forced himself to answer her questions, even managed to ask after her health and that of the wild, arrogant

Greek who was her husband, before he extricated himself from the unwanted conversation, switched off the phone and lay back against the pillows again, closing his eyes with a heartfelt sigh of relief.

It was only then that he noticed a change in the position of the woman beside him.

Caitlin no longer lay relaxed and warm and deeply, luxuriously asleep at his side. She had moved, turning over slightly, so that she was lying on her back. And her slender frame was no longer curved close to his but held stiffly and tautly straight, a calculated distance across the sheet away.

It was that and a subtle change in the quality of the silence in the room that warned him. The absolute stillness in the way she lay, and some secret sixth sense that told him she was no longer asleep, but very definitely awake, and with her head turned in his direction, watching him.

And that was when he remembered.

Rhys Morgan.

He had answered the phone without thinking, switching it on and giving, as he always did, his name.

His *real* name.

'Oh, damn,' he muttered under his breath. 'Oh, damn, damn, *damn*!'

As he forced himself to open his eyes and meet the blaze of fury, the burning reproach in those molten golden eyes, he knew that there was no way back.

She knew.

She knew exactly who he was and why he was here.

And now all hell was very definitely going to break loose. And there was nothing he could do to stop it.

CHAPTER SIX

'GET out!'

She didn't shout, she didn't even raise her voice above a conversational tone, but she used the words with such deadly intent that Rhys felt the sting of them more than any more openly furious attack.

'*Rhys Morgan*— You're Rhys— *Get out!* Get out of my bed, out of my home and out of my life!'

'No.'

It was the weirdest situation he had ever been in. Lying there naked under the bedclothes, with an equally naked woman only inches away, her brown hair still tumbled and tousled from their lovemaking in the night, her lips still swollen from the shared passion of their kisses—and with her golden eyes spitting hatred at him.

'I'm not going anywhere until we've talked this out.'

'And I'm not talking to you about *anything*! Get out!'

'Look, can't we be civilised about this?'

'Civilised?'

The word was a sound of pure disbelief. Of total, absolute rejection of even the hope of a possible discussion or anything coming close to peace negotiations. She wasn't even prepared to listen. And he knew that he shouldn't blame her.

She had every right to be furious. To hate the deception he had practised on her. And he could see that fury, that hatred in her expression right now. He'd been prepared for that, and could handle it.

But what he hadn't expected, and couldn't cope with

anything like as well, was the bitter sense of betrayal that was there right under the fury. Betrayal was the last thing he had expected her to feel and it didn't square well with his conscience at all.

'Can you tell me what is *civilised* about lying your way into my life—into my bed—into my body? And taking them without a second thought. Using me for your own selfish pleasure and then discarding—'

'No!'

He couldn't allow her to follow that line of thought. He could be accused of a lot of things, things he didn't want to look at too closely right now, but that was not one of them.

'That isn't true and you know it! I never used you! If you want to be strictly accurate then we—'

'Oh, yes,' Caitlin cut in with bitter cynicism. 'Let's be *strictly accurate* by all means. I suppose you're going to tell me that we used each other.'

'Well, didn't we?' Rhys flung back. 'From where I was standing the whole thing was definitely mutual. You're not trying to claim that I forced you—or even put undue pressure on you?'

That took something of the angry fight out of her, making her shield the blazing eyes behind hooded lids, white teeth worrying at the fullness of her bottom lip.

'No,' she admitted reluctantly. 'No, I'm not saying you *forced me*—'

'Good.'

'But...'

'But what?' Rhys prompted unwisely when she hesitated for a moment.

Unwisely because his interjection brought the anger flaring again, turning her eyes molten as they looked up and burned into his.

'But you sure as hell didn't tell me the truth, and that means you got yourself into my...my bed under false pretences.'

He didn't like the way that made him sound—or the way it made him feel.

'If we're talking about the truth, lady, then the *truth* is that you didn't give a damn who I was last night. You wouldn't have cared if my name is Matthew Delaney—'

'Which it isn't!'

'Which it is—Rhys Matthew Delaney Morgan! So at least I have more right to the name than you have to my daughter!'

There, it was out. At last the real truth was out in the open. But strangely he didn't feel any better for it. In fact, seeing the way she flinched back against the pillows twisted something savagely inside. He just wished his damn conscience wasn't quite so touchy.

After all, she was the one who had started all this by keeping his daughter from him.

'Your...'

Abruptly she caught herself up, shaking her head faintly.

'I should have known that was what this was all about.'

Her voice was low, flat, empty of emotion, and her eyes had lost all the fire of just moments before, looking shockingly dull and clouded.

'Of course that was what this was all about. You don't think that when I heard, I would have just shrugged off the idea that I had a kid and said, Oh, well, I hope she's happy with whoever has her—with this cousin that I've never met and I don't know from Adam.'

'Who told you?'

'A friend. And what does it matter who the hell told me? That child is my baby. My daughter—and you kept her from me. You...'

How had he come to be leaning over her like this, raging into her face while she tried to shrink even further back down into the mattress, pulling the sheets right up to her chin? Dear God, she had got him so furious that he had forgotten the most basic facts about the way he believed it was right to behave.

'I'm sorry,' he muttered roughly and unwillingly, and forced himself back to his own side of the bed.

She was not appeased.

'Get out!' she said again, with more force and infinitely more venom than before. 'I said get out!'

'I know what you said, but if that's your only answer to everything, then it isn't going to work.'

'Are you going to get out of here?'

'No.'

It was his turn to lean back against the pillows, but this time his arms were folded tight across his chest and his eyes threatened her with all sorts of retribution if she dared to risk trying to move him.

'I'm going nowhere until I see my child. If you can't stand the heat—then get out yourself.'

'All right.'

She flung back the covers, swung her legs to the side, then paused and turned to glare at him furiously.

'You might at least have the decency to look away.'

'Why?'

Black fury wasn't the best foundation for perfect manners and he didn't feel like being polite. He was furious at the way that she hadn't acknowledged that she'd been the one in the wrong, keeping his daughter from him. But then, what had he expected? That she would suddenly come over all repentant and beg him to forgive her?

'There's nothing I haven't seen before—I paid very close attention last night.'

The fiery wash of colour that flooded her cheeks revealed just how much he had needled her.

'That was under very different circumstances!'

'We're still the same people.'

'No,' she muttered, low and fierce. 'No, you're not at all the person I thought you were. You're light-years away from being him.'

And after one last searing glare from those wild cat's eyes, she got to her feet, and stalked, holding herself tall and proud, her head arrogantly high, round the side of the bed and across the room to the door to the bathroom.

She had courage, he had to give her that. After that one burning look, she allowed herself no sign of discomfort or embarrassment at knowing that he was watching her. Even the hot colour had fled from her face, leaving her cool and, outwardly at least, calmly in control as she walked past him.

'I'm going to take a shower. A very long, very hot shower.'

The tone of her voice expressed only too clearly the way she felt—that she wanted to wash off his touch and the feel of his hands and every other part of his body that had been close to her in the night.

'If you have any decency at all, then you'll get dressed and be gone by the time I come out.'

She didn't quite slam the door behind her, but the firm way it was closed had a finality all of its own.

Decency be damned, Rhys told himself, still staring hard at the white-painted wood that had come between them. He wasn't going anywhere. He'd said he was staying here until he saw his daughter and he meant it.

He was staying, and if that meant fighting dirty with Ms Caitlin 'Get out of my life' Richardson, then that was the way he'd have to go.

Though it was a great pity.

The thought caught him sharply by surprise, making him shift uncomfortably beneath the covers.

So they had shared a great night together. A hot, hungry night. He had experienced some of the greatest, most fulfilling sex he had ever known—bar none. But was that a reason to start going soft on her? To start wondering if there could be more to it—maybe even a future?

'A *future* be damned!'

Now it was his turn to throw back the covers and fling himself out of the bed. He was too restless to lie there, in the bed they had shared, with the perfume of Caitlin's skin and hair still saturating the sheets and the pillows.

Was he going soft? Totally out of his head? Could he even want to consider a future with the woman who had connived with his wife to keep his baby from him? Who would have kept the child for herself if he hadn't found out by accident?

No way!

And yet—and yet...

Through the door he could hear the sound of the water rushing in the shower and the images it conjured up had him prowling restlessly round the room, gathering up his scattered clothing, too uneasy to stay still.

She might need a hot shower, but he needed a cold, cold one—cold enough to freeze his thoughts as well as his body.

He had to get dressed—or at least pull on his trousers if nothing else. Perhaps then his mind would stay strictly on the straight and narrow and not keep wandering off to memories of just how wonderful Caitlin had looked just now as she'd stalked past him, head high, graceful and proud. And totally defiant in her nakedness.

All he'd wanted was to grab her and get her back into bed with him and make mad, passionate love to her.

And the dangerous words in there were *mad* and *love*. Because he would have to be totally mad to do it. He had been crazy enough last night, but this morning things were so much more complicated, and he could just imagine Caitlin's reaction if he'd so much as tried it. And there was nothing even remotely like *love* in what he felt. It was another, totally different four-letter word.

Lust, and only that.

Lust had been what he had felt for Amelie. Lust that he had so foolishly, so naïvely mistaken for something deeper, longer-lasting—permanent. He had felt lust but he'd acted as if he were in love, and look where that had got him.

No. Wanting this woman came with too many entanglements, he told himself as he pulled on his trousers and zipped them up with a ferocious determination. He'd taken too many risks last night as it was. From now on that hunger was going to have to be put aside, kept permanently under lock and key.

It was as he reached for his jacket that the realisation of just how stupid he had been came home to him with a force that rocked his sense of reality, making him groan aloud.

'Oh, no. Oh, hellfire…'

His hand had only brushed against the pocket, feeling the faint outline of the shape inside, but he didn't need any further information, any more proof. The box of condoms that he had slipped into his jacket pocket before last leaving his room, just in case, was still there. Exactly where he had left it. Still completely unopened. Still totally unused.

'Hell and damnation! No!'

What had he done now?

From the bathroom the sound of the still running shower

made him turn his head and stare hard at the firmly locked door.

'Oh, Caitlin, Caitlin, is it too much to hope that *you* were prepared? That you were protected?'

But with her in this mood, hating him as she did, how was he going to manage to ask her that all-important question? And wasn't it too late for questions anyway?

What the hell was he going to do if the answer was no?

Caitlin had no idea how long she had been standing under the shower, letting the hot water pound down onto her head and body. She didn't know and she didn't care. The only thing that registered in her thoughts was the belief that she would never, ever feel clean again.

She felt sullied, dirtied—*used*.

And so desperately, desperately betrayed.

How had she let it happen again?

How had she let herself come close to a man, come to start feeling, start *caring* for him, only to find herself totally let down? Totally deceived.

Totally destroyed.

Last night she had felt so wanted. So needed. For the first time since Josh had told her that he no longer loved her, that he had fallen for Amelie like a ton of bricks, she had actually found herself coming out of the protective cocoon in which she had been hiding as a result. She had let herself feel an interest in, a need for another man.

She had let herself care for him enough to go to bed with him. They had made love together, not once, but many many times...

'No!' She said the word aloud. It seemed to have more force that way.

But the truth was that no force in the world would wipe

away what had happened. Just as no amount of hot water would ever wash away the feeling of being used.

'Making love—ha!'

Reaching up, she switched off the hot-water flow with a snap of her wrist, finally admitting that standing here in the shower was getting her nowhere at all.

'Making love had nothing to do with it,' she muttered, scrubbing at her face and hair with a towel. 'It was sex and nothing more. Sex pure and simple.'

Unprotected sex.

'Oh, *no*! Please, no!'

If she had suddenly turned the shower gauge to 'Cold' and deluged herself in water that was the temperature of ice, she couldn't have shocked herself more thoroughly or more devastatingly.

Unprotected sex.

She had had sex—she refused to honour it with any other name—with Rhys Morgan last night. So many times that she had lost count. And not once in any of those hot, passionate—go on, yes, admit it—*fulfilling* sessions had either of them used any form of contraception.

Clutching at the side of the basin, Caitlin sank down onto the toilet seat, her legs having the consistency of jelly beneath her.

What if…?

Oh, dear God, what would she do if last night had consequences? Permanent consequences. Because if she was to be pregnant—by *Rhys Morgan* of all people—then there was no way she could abort any baby she had conceived. Even one that had a father like that man. And if she…

But no, she was tormenting herself with things she couldn't deal with yet because they were still totally in the realms of 'What if?' She had enough to cope with right now.

The silence from her bedroom allowed her the chance of a little hope that maybe, just maybe, Rhys had done as she asked and gone. She was going to have to risk it anyway, because she couldn't stay in here all day long. It was getting late as it was. Her father was going to start ringing or, worse, calling round to find out where she was if she didn't put in an appearance soon. She'd left him alone with Fleur quite long enough.

Reaching for the peach-coloured velvet robe that hung behind the bathroom door, she pulled it on, belted it tightly around her waist, drew in a much needed breath, straightened her shoulders and opened the door.

Her hopes were dashed immediately.

Rhys Morgan was lounging in a chair, half-dressed and apparently totally at his ease.

'You're still here!'

'As you can see.'

'But I told you to go.'

'And I told you that I wasn't going anywhere until I see my daughter. I came here to find my child and I'm not leaving without her.'

'Well, tough!'

Marching across to the wardrobe, she pulled out clothes at random, not caring what her hand fell on. Anything would do; anything at all. The only thing that mattered was getting *dressed*. Covering herself in something—anything. Protecting herself from this man's cold blue eyes.

Though the truth was that, the way he was glaring at her right now, she felt that she'd need a suit of armour to defend herself from that searing stare.

'I have work to do. I need to get dressed.'

'And we're going through that whole ''Little Miss Modesty'' pantomime again, are we?' Rhys taunted, but then, suddenly and totally unexpectedly, he pushed himself to his feet.

'I'd feel better for a shower myself, if you don't mind if I use the bathroom.'

'Be my guest.'

She didn't know if he had suddenly had an attack of conscience or had decided that tact was the best approach—or if, quite simply, like her he felt decidedly grubby after last night. But she was just so grateful for the opportunity to have a few minutes alone that she would have run a bath for him if need be.

'There are clean towels in the airing cupboard.'

Having him shut the door behind him brought such a rush of relief that she almost sank down on the carpet in weak exhaustion. Only the thought that she had no idea how long he was going to take, and the realisation that her time of privacy might be very short-lived, kept her upright and determined. The last thing she needed was for Rhys to open the door and find her still in her underwear.

Hurrying into a neat white T-shirt and navy trousers, she yanked a comb through her hair, pulling the still wet strands back into a smooth pony-tail. She didn't feel like prettying up in any way, but self-esteem demanded that at least she didn't face the world showing every second of her near-sleepless night in the pallor of her face, the faint shadows under her eyes.

A quick smoothing of tinted moisturiser into her skin, a touch of lipstick and a slick of mascara onto her lashes made things look slightly better. There was no time for anything more as the rush of water in the shower was shut off and the knowledge that Rhys was on his way out had her hurrying from the room and down the stairs.

Anything other than to face the prospect of seeing him emerge from the bathroom, his lean torso still faintly warm from the shower, the crisp dark hair flattened to the strong bones of his skull by the water.

Food was the last thing she wanted, but she made a pot of rich, strong coffee in the hope that it would wake her up a little, stimulate her bewildered brain cells into thinking of some way out of this mess. She still hadn't come up with anything by the time she heard Rhys's footsteps descending the stairs and he came to stand in the doorway, leaning idly against the wooden frame.

'The coffee smells good,' he commented with a relaxed casualness that only added to her sense of discomposure and being on edge.

Why wasn't he as ill-at-ease as she felt? Couldn't he at least have the decency to look just a little bit less sure of himself? But then, of course, he was probably only too used to waking up in strange beds with relatively unknown women by his side. Quite unlike herself, who had only ever known Josh in that way—until now.

'There's some in the pot—help yourself.'

It was an effort to force her voice into speech but she managed it.

'Thanks…'

This time there was a little less confidence in his tone, and, hearing it, Caitlin looked up from studying her own mug of coffee to see that he hadn't moved. Instead, he was still in the doorway, but this time he was studying her intently as if he had something uncomfortable on his mind.

And the thought that it might just be every bit as uncomfortable as what was on *her* mind pushed her into unguarded speech.

'It's not poisoned! However much I might wish you had never come into my life, I'm not so desperate as to take that way out.'

His grin in response was quick, wry and bleakly cynical.

'You might want to when you hear what I have to say.'

CHAPTER SEVEN

CAITLIN was proud of her response.

Other than a quick tightening of her grip on the handle of her mug, until her knuckles showed white, she managed to maintain a degree of control that might have seemed like calm if you didn't look too closely at the shadows in her eyes, the way that the colour had fled from her cheeks.

'Is this the point where you say the line about "we didn't use anything"?'

Rhys nodded, his face grim.

'Unfortunately.'

He levered himself upright, crossed the room to the worktop where the coffee-pot stood, and poured himself a mug of the dark brew. But all the time his brilliant blue eyes stayed fixed on her face, watching every fleeting change of expression that flickered across it.

'Don't let it trouble you. I won't.'

She had hoped to sound unconcerned and reassuring but failed miserably. Instead she just came across as coldly indifferent, stupidly careless.

'That's a totally irresponsible attitude!'

'Oh, is it?'

Lightning flashes of anger flared in the burnt amber of her eyes, defying him openly.

'And who are you to lecture me about irresponsibility when you weren't exactly thinking twice about *precautions* last night? I didn't notice you putting on any brakes, saying hang on—'

'All right!'

For the first time since she had known him, Rhys's voice came close to a shout as he slammed his coffee mug down on the worktop so violently that the brown liquid slopped over the sides. But almost immediately he seemed to recollect himself, ruthlessly reigning in the black fury that burned in his eyes.

Drawing a deep, ragged breath, he spoke more calmly. 'OK, I admit I wasn't thinking either. But if you had been—if you'd once said stop, or that you weren't protected...'

'So now it's all my fault? You didn't want any of it?'

'Of course I did—then! But now I'm deeply regretting something that I wish had never, ever happened.'

Oh, he knew how to stick the knife in, Caitlin reflected miserably. How to slide an emotional stiletto right in between her ribs and then twist it sharply until she almost screamed in agony.

Deeply regretting something that I wish had never, ever happened.

Yes, he knew how to reduce something that she had thought was so wonderful, so special, the hope of a new beginning, to a quick tumble in a stranger's bed. Something so sordid and meaningless that he already regretted it had ever happened.

'Well, don't worry about it.'

Again she tried to sound confident, only managing the sort of airy indifference that earned her another savage glare of dark reproof.

'No, honestly—wrong time of the month.'

He looked so relieved that she wanted to throw what was left of her coffee right in his face. And she would have done if she hadn't known deep down inside that she was lying and it was nothing like the *wrong* time of the month, unless of course you meant the wrong time of the month to be having wild, crazy, totally unprotected sex with a near complete stranger. And that it very definitely had been.

Not that there ever was a *right* time for the lunatic way she had behaved last night.

'Are you sure?'

'Well, I can't guarantee it. But I don't think you need to concern yourself about the possible consequences of our stupidity.'

'I can't not concern myself. I was involved.'

'Look, I'll see the doctor. This is the sort of situation the morning-after pill is made for. It will be fine.'

'Well, if you should have any doubts then you'll let me know.'

Not 'please let me know'—or even 'you should let me know'. But 'you'll let me know' as a command, an order that he expected to have obeyed.

'And you will…?'

'Well, naturally, I'll take care of my responsibilities.'

'Naturally.'

Suddenly too uneasy and uncomfortable to stay where she was, with those cold blue eyes watching her every expression, she moved across the kitchen, silent on bare feet, to perch on a pinewood stool beside the small breakfast bar, tucking her feet up on the first rung.

'And you needn't worry about anything else. Any infection…'

Rhys seemed determined to rub her nose in the totally sordid side of the events of the previous night.

'There will be no problem there.'

'Oh. Great. That's good to know.'

She flashed a weak, insincere mockery of a smile on and off like a neon sign, and pretended to drink some of her coffee, grimacing as she realised that it was now almost completely cold.

Well, if she'd had any illusions left that last night had meant something—anything—to him then he'd completely demolished them in a few short, blunt sentences.

Totally irresponsible…

Something that I wish had never, ever happened…

Naturally, I'll take care of my responsibilities…

You needn't worry about anything else. Any infection…

The words pounded against her skull like blows, making her want to cover her head with her hands and moan aloud. As it was, she closed her eyes for a moment so that she didn't have to look into Rhys's cold, brutal face.

He hadn't left her with a shred of self-respect or pride— but that wasn't the worst thing about this whole appalling situation.

The worst thing was knowing that he had come for Fleur. That the baby was what he wanted. And that, if he could, he would take the little girl away from her.

And leave her with nothing.

In the darkness behind her closed lids she suddenly heard Rhys draw in his breath sharply and rawly.

'Caitlin…'

Something about his use of her name penetrated the fog of misery that shrouded Caitlin's mind, forcing itself on her attention. Some sudden, dramatic change in his tone of voice, an unexpected, totally bewildering note of sharp concern alerting her to the fact that he was suddenly in a very different mood.

'Dear God, Caitlin, what's wrong? What's happened to you?'

'Wrong?'

She couldn't help herself; her eyes flew open, looking straight into the dark, shadowed concern of his.

Had she got him all wrong? Had she misread a sign or two somewhere? Was it possible that he actually really *cared* after all? That she mattered at least just a little bit to him?

'Wh—what do you mean, what's wrong?' she quavered, afraid of letting show just how much this change of heart meant, and at the same time afraid that he might think it didn't matter at all.

But Rhys's sapphire eyes were fixed on a point much lower than her pale, strained face. He was staring at—

Fearfully she followed the line of his gaze down past her waist, her knees, her legs, to the point where...

'Oh!'

Seeing what he'd seen, she couldn't hold back the cry of shock and concern. Her left foot was bleeding, red stains were smudged and painted all over the white skin of her instep and above. And on the beige tiles of the kitchen floor, little red drops marked everywhere she had stood, tracing out her path with perfect clarity.

'What the hell have you done?' His tone was a disturbing blend of exasperation and concern.

'I—don't know.'

Shaken, Caitlin held out her foot, watching in shocked fascination as another tiny drop of blood trickled along the edge of the sole.

'What...?'

Instantly she regretted her action as Rhys slammed down his coffee mug and came towards her. To her horror he dropped to one knee before her, taking her bare foot in cool, solicitous hands and turning it gently so that he could examine it closely.

'What's happened?'

'The photo frame upstairs,' Rhys pronounced. 'The broken glass. You must have stood on that when you were getting dressed. Didn't you notice?'

'N-no. Not really.'

Wasn't the truth more that she had been so totally uptight, so severely stressed out, that she hadn't been capable
of noticing—or feeling—anything? She had been so hor-
rified by what she had just learned about Rhys, completely
obsessed with just what this meant and the possible reper-
cussions of the discovery, that she couldn't form any other
thought in her mind. She must have cut her foot then and
simply not even realised.

'It looks worse than it is.'

Rhys was examining the sole of her foot, studying it
closely and touching it carefully in several places. The in-
describably gentle sensation of his fingers against her lac-
erated skin made Caitlin draw in her breath on a raw, uneven sigh.

Instantly his dark head came up sharply, blue eyes lock-
ing with burning gold.

'Am I hurting you?'

Caitlin could only shake her head in fierce desperation,
willing him to believe her. She felt the colour ebb and flow
in her face and could only pray that he thought the discomfort in her foot was responsible for her uncontrolled reaction.

She couldn't bear it if he guessed what it meant to her
to have this devastating, arrogant man kneeling before her,
her wounded foot held gently in his strong hands, his proud
dark head bent over it. She could inhale the scent of his
skin, see the dark shadow on his strong jawline where he
was desperately in need of a shave, and the temptation to
reach out and stroke the soft black silk of his hair was
almost overwhelming.

Last night, or, rather, the events of the morning, the rev-
elation of who he was and the total indifference he had
shown to her feelings as a result, should have taught her
that she was playing with fire even dreaming of being in-

volved with a man like Rhys. Common sense screamed at her that to be involved with him was only flirting with danger. She didn't *want* to be involved with him. But when he came up close to her like this and touched her so gently, his blue eyes darkening with what seemed like genuine concern, she knew that all the 'shoulds' and all the common sense in the world had no impact on the way she *felt*.

And the way she felt was that if Rhys Morgan was to look up into her face as he had done then and say, 'Caitlin, I want you. Come back to bed with me again and let me make love to you over and over, all through the rest of the day and long into the night,' then she would go with him, foolishly and blindly maybe, but oh, so willingly and oh, so happily.

And then? How would she deal with the result? The fallout from her own emotional equivalent of a nuclear war?

But of course Rhys didn't say those words. He didn't tell her he wanted her. He didn't ask her to come back to bed with him. Instead he frowned over the small wounds in her foot, examining them closely.

'There are some tiny bits of glass in here. You've been walking round like this all morning?'

'Hardly all morning!' Caitlin protested, the contrast between the words her imagination had put into his mouth and the ones he actually spoke twisting her up inside. 'It's only been a short time!'

'Long enough.'

Rhys knew that he was speaking roughly, that he sounded far more angry than sympathetic, but he seemed to have lost control of his voice. He had no idea what it was about this woman that made his normally firm grip on his self-control weaken so badly. He only knew that when he was with her his thoughts became scrambled and opaque and he just wasn't functioning normally.

Or, rather, one part of him was functioning in overdrive, he admitted, while the rest, the more rational parts, seemed to have lost all their power. Uncomfortably he shifted from one knee to another, trying to ignore the ache in his groin and disguise the blatant evidence of just what being here, like this, was doing to him. The movement tightened his grip on Caitlin's foot and instinctively she jerked slightly away from him.

'Hold still, woman!' he growled, flashing her a furious glare.

'I am holding still!' she protested. 'You're the one who moved.'

'I have to see this in the light.'

He shifted again, under the pretext of turning her foot towards the window, but it did no good. The heat and pressure below his waist remained just as troublesome, not easing a bit.

How could just holding her foot do this to him?

The long, narrow bones were delicate in his hands, the fine, soft skin intensely pale against the deeper colour of his fingers. The curve of her heel fitted into the palm of his hand with a sensual perfection and the shadowy cleft between the big toe and the one next to it was an unnerving echo of the perfumed valley of her cleavage in the deep turquoise lace bra as he had undressed her the previous night.

He had to fight himself hard not to give in to the temptation to lift her foot to his lips and press a kiss onto each and every one of those toes, before moving along the curve of her instep, to her ankle…

Oh, hell, no! No. Thinking this way was only making things so much worse.

'You need this cleaning up and some antiseptic putting on it. Do you have a first-aid box?'

'Bottom cupboard on the left.'

She gestured with a nod, sending the long pony-tail in which she'd fastened her hair flying.

Her voice had sounded almost as strained as his, Rhys couldn't help thinking as, thankful for the momentary respite, he got up from his place on the floor and hunted in the cupboard she'd indicated. Was it possible that she was feeling this as badly as him?

She certainly looked pale enough, those amazing eyes shadowed and clouded.

It helped to concentrate on practical matters like hot water and cotton wool and Elastoplast so that by the time he was back in his kneeling position on the floor he felt that he could cope this time.

If he was quick.

If he didn't look up into her face and think about how it had felt to kiss those lips where now white teeth were worrying at the fullness of the bottom one. And didn't think about last night as he wiped away the trickle of blood that had run down her heel.

Last night, when those long, slender legs had curled around his waist so tightly that her heels had rested on the backs of his thighs and she had...

Hell, not again!

He rubbed rather more roughly at her foot in an attempt to distract his thoughts, causing Caitlin to draw in her breath sharply between her teeth.

'I'm sorry—nearly done.'

And he couldn't be finished soon enough, he told himself. He did *not* want to feel this way. In fact, he wanted to feel anything but.

He had come downstairs this morning, determined to have things out with Caitlin. To tell her a few home truths, and put his cards on the table. And the first thing he'd planned on was making only too plain just what an appalling mistake he'd—they'd—made getting into bed together. A mistake that must never, ever be repeated. And then he was going to demand that she hand over his daughter.

He'd done quite well on the first point. And she'd even helped him by making it plain that she felt the same way. That the last thing she wanted was a repetition of the madness that had gripped them last night. They had both seemed totally in agreement on that at least. And if he could only have gone on to talk about the baby…

But then he'd been distracted by the injury to her foot.

How *could* he have let himself be diverted from his main, his only purpose in being here?

How could he have forgotten about his child, his daughter, when she was the one thing that had brought him here in the first place?

'There.'

He placed the last strip of protective plaster over one of the larger cuts and stuck it down, smoothing it tightly over the pale skin.

'That's that done. Finished.'

'Thank you.'

She sounded subdued, thoughtful, but he wasn't going to allow himself to wonder what was going through her mind. What he needed was to concentrate on what was important—what really mattered.

'No problem.'

Screwing the protective paper from the plaster up into a ball and lobbing it vaguely in the direction of the bin, he let her foot go abruptly and stood up, taking the bowl of water to the sink to empty it out.

'Anyone would have done it. I couldn't leave you bleeding all over the floor. No, wait,' he commanded as she started to get to her feet. 'You can't wander about like that. At least let me get you some shoes—or slippers?'

Caitlin subsided back onto the chair, clearly not liking his abrupt tone.

'In the cloakroom—by the door.'

It was just the break he needed. Just enough time to draw in a deep, calming breath and force his mind away from the sultry, erotic paths it had been following and on to calmer, more important matters.

And so had she.

'Rhys, we have to talk about the baby,' she began as soon as he came back into the room.

'There's nothing to talk about,' he declared, dropping the shoes on the floor at her feet without ceremony. 'I came here to get her and I'm not leaving without her. That's all there is to say.'

It wasn't all *she* had to say, Caitlin reflected uneasily, trying to push her feet into her shoes without dislodging the plasters or catching one of the tiny cuts on the leather. But she didn't know how or where to begin.

Whatever she said, he wasn't going to like it. And there was one major detail that she knew he was just going to hate. One that she didn't have the faintest idea how to start telling him.

'It isn't that simple...'

'It's perfectly simple.'

Not listening, the expression on his face said. *And you're not going to persuade me to listen unless you go along with what I want.*

'I want my baby, Caitlin. Amelie's and my child. That's why I came here.'

'Rhys, please—let me tell you about—'

'*No!*'

It was brutally cold, icily emphatic. No argument, no debate, just this one forceful syllable.

'I don't want you to tell me anything about my baby! I don't want to *hear* anything second-hand. I want to see her—to hold her—to get to know her myself. One to one—with no in-between. That's the way I want it and that's the way it's going to be.'

'Amelie didn't want you to have her.'

'Amelie was a selfish bitch and a liar!' Rhys exploded. 'She told you I wanted her to have an abortion—is that right?'

'Y-yes…'

Caitlin was struggling to recognise the man who stood before her. The charming, urbane companion who had shared her dinner table, the passionate lover of the night before, had vanished. Even the coolly distant man of just moments before was transformed into this coldly angry creature whose eyes blazed blue fire, and whose beautiful mouth had white marks of blind fury etched strongly around it.

If *this* Rhys had been her cousin's husband, then she could see exactly why Amelie had left in the first place.

'No,' Rhys stated harshly, 'it's not true—not a word of it. I didn't tell Amelie to have an abortion. *She* told *me* that if she ever got pregnant she was having one. She had never wanted children, and she couldn't stand the thought of getting fat and ugly—she'd do anything rather than go through that. That's why we split up the first time—she ran away from me and from the thought of ever being a mother.'

'I don't believe you!'

She couldn't believe him. It couldn't be true. Any of it. How could it when Amelie had told her the opposite? And Josh…

'So you think your cousin was such a saint? You said yourself you didn't know her.'

'I didn't, but—'

'But what?'

How could she tell him? How could she let him know the truth about this baby he thought was his when he had come so far, determined to find her? How could she tell him the real truth when he could only hate it—and hate her all the more for revealing it to him?

And the shocking thing was that she didn't know which felt worse—the thought of the pain the truth would bring to him, or the idea of him detesting her even more than he clearly did already.

'Caitlin…'

Rhys's voice held an ominous note of warning, the promise of retribution if she didn't explain herself—and fast.

'I don't— I know…'

Desperately she floundered, not knowing which way to turn, how to phrase it, what to say…

But then, just as she drew in a fearful breath, ready to try and speak, a sudden rap at the door startled them both.

While they were still standing, frozen in shock, there was the sound of a key in the lock, the door was pushed open, and a cheery female voice echoed round the tiny hallway.

'Cait? You there? Is everything OK?'

Mandy, Caitlin thought bitterly. Sweet, helpful Mandy, who worked as a chambermaid in the hotel and who adored children. Who often acted as babysitter…Panic clutched at her throat, holding her silent and still when she most wished she could move or say something—anything.

'Your dad was worried when it was getting so late and you hadn't turned up. So he sent me over with a key.'

Please let her be alone, Caitlin prayed. Please, please, let her be alone…

But even as she sent the desperate entreaty heavenwards she could hear Mandy stepping into the hallway, the slight grunt she made indicating that the older woman was carrying something—or someone. And at the same time her listening ears caught the faint snuffling beginnings that experience told her would swiftly change into a full-throated cry.

She didn't dare to look into Rhys's face, to watch him turn, see his reaction, as with the worst timing possible the baby he was seeking announced her arrival at the top of her voice.

CHAPTER EIGHT

RHYS was the first to recover.

While Caitlin still stood frozen to the spot, staring wide-eyed in shock and disbelief, it was Rhys who moved forward, switching on a ready, charming smile that clearly had exactly the effect he wanted.

Mandy melted like ice in the sun just at the sight of it.

'Hi,' he said smoothly. 'I'm Rhys—I'm afraid I'm the reason why Caitlin's been delayed so long. I'm sorry about that.'

'No problem.' Mandy's eyes were huge with astonished delight and she was practically drooling.

Oh, great! And now the whole hotel staff would know that Rhys Morgan had spent the night here, Caitlin thought bitterly. Knowing how much Mandy loved to gossip, she clearly couldn't wait until she got back and told everyone all about it.

'And you're—?'

'Mandy.'

'OK, Mandy—let me take the little one from you...'

No!

The word screamed inside Caitlin's head but she didn't dare give voice to it. For one thing she didn't want to frighten the little girl. And for another, she was afraid that any false move on her part might just push Rhys into reckless action. The door was still wide open behind them, the car park only a few metres away. If he decided to turn and go with the baby neither Mandy nor she would be able to stop him. He could be in his car and gone...

Swallowing hard, she forced herself to find the strength to speak.

'I'll take her…'

'No, it's fine,' Rhys dismissed her feeble croak with a single arrogant glance. 'I have her.'

I have her, and I'm going to keep her, his tone said only too clearly to Caitlin's over-sensitive ears. Or was that just her desperate feeling of horror, the result of tightly stretched nerves, distorting her hearing? Mandy didn't appear to find anything wrong at all but handed over the shawl-wrapped bundle without a qualm.

'She doesn't like strangers,' Caitlin tried again.

Then watched in despair as the baby blithely proved her wrong by not only stopping the petulant wail she had been indulging in, but also settling down into Rhys's arms as if she had been born to be there. The tiny head, covered in downy dark hair, rested securely in the crook of the man's strong arm, and her wide blue eyes blinked once, then stared up into his face in apparently fascinated delight.

'Hello, little one,' Rhys murmured, and the softness of his tone caught on something desperately raw and painful in Caitlin's heart and twisted a brutal knife agonisingly where it was already wounded.

Through the blood that was pounding in her head, she heard Mandy say something, though what she had no idea, but she nodded all the same. Dimly she was aware of the other woman turning, leaving, and shutting the door behind her, but she didn't see her go.

The only thing she could see, the one thing that held her gaze, was the tall, dark, stunning man before her. The big man and the tiny baby held so securely in his arms. And that, the one thing she had prayed that she would never, ever see, was all that her stunned vision could focus on, seeing it with an excruciating clarity.

She had never seen anyone fall in love before, but now she watched and saw it happen right before her eyes. She watched Rhys Morgan look down into the small, upturned face of the baby girl he believed was his daughter, and lose his heart to her, put his soul in thrall in the space of a heartbeat.

He didn't say a word. He didn't have to. He just looked and smiled.

Smiled in a way that she had never, ever seen on his hard features before. In a way that said his devotion had been won, given totally and freely. Handed over without a second thought and with no hope of return. He wouldn't care about that anyway.

It was as if she had ceased to be. As if she had faded from existence, into total oblivion, and the man and the baby were the only things in the room. And they were totally absorbed in each other.

Because Fleur too seemed transfixed. She had lost all her normal shyness and unease with people she didn't know. She had even forgotten the nagging beginnings of hunger which had started the crabby wailing of just a few moments before and which normally went on and on until her appetite was appeased. She just lay there and stared up at the strong male face above her and blew tiny bubbles of delight from her rosebud-pink lips.

'What's her name?'

It didn't sound like Rhys's voice. In fact it sounded so unlike anything she had ever heard from him before that she blinked hard, actually looking round the room to see if anyone else had come into the house while she had been standing, stunned and mesmerised by the scene before her.

Of course there was no one.

'What?'

The struggle to force it out made the word crack embarrassingly in the middle, her voice too not sounding like her own. She didn't need to ask the question either. She knew exactly what he had said; she just couldn't cope with the question—with any questions—when she couldn't work out just what the significance of them, and her answers, might be.

'Caitlin!'

Rhys's note of warning was deliberately pitched so that it was strong enough to be heard but would do nothing to disturb the little girl in his arms. And Fleur didn't even blink but went on staring, holding the man's blue-eyed gaze with an effortless calm.

'What's her name?'

She didn't dare to ignore it a second time.

'Fleur,' she whispered, her voice no more than a thin thread of sound that he must have had to strain hard to hear. 'Her name is Fleur.'

'Fleur.'

It was just a sigh. A crooning sound of soft delight that clawed brutally at the already raw wound in her heart just to hear it.

It was a sound she had never thought she would hear— never, ever wanted to hear. A sound that undermined everything she had believed up to now. That put violent explosives under the walls she had built up around herself, set light to the fast-burning fuse that led straight to them.

It made a mockery of everything Amelie had ever said. And turned her cousin's story into a lie in the blink of an eye.

At least the part of the story where Rhys Morgan was concerned.

No man who had ever wanted his wife to abort their child, no man who had ever declared that he didn't want children would ever take to a small baby with such ease and warmth. So Amelie must have made things up. She had to have done.

But if that part was true—what about the rest of the story? The one that Josh had told her?

Caitlin didn't know what to think. And she didn't know where to look for an answer.

Not from the man in front of her. The man who was so absorbed in the baby that nothing would distract him.

So absorbed that she doubted he would even hear the truth if she tried to tell him.

But *was* it the truth?

There was no one she could turn to for the answer to that. The only people who could tell her the real truth were both dead, and she didn't know if they could be trusted anyway.

There was just one thing she did know, and that was that she couldn't risk telling Rhys Morgan any of it. Not right now. Not when he had Fleur in his hands, his strong arms holding her so safely.

And he was still smiling that damn smile.

'Fleur,' he crooned in a soft voice that turned her insides to water. *'Ma petite Fleur.'*

Oh, damn, now tears were pricking at her eyes, blurring her vision. She couldn't let this go on. Had to stop it somehow.

'Mandy…' she tried then stopped abruptly, her voice behaving in the most peculiar way. It had shot up to an appalling squeak on the word, cracking embarrassingly at the last moment.

Caitlin swallowed hard, trying to get control back.

'Mandy brought her round because it's getting close to her next feed time,' she managed, with rather more clarity this time. 'She'll be getting hungry any minute.'

Damn you, Fleur, at least you could *look* just a tiny bit

hungry! she reproved the little girl privately. Normally by this time of the day the baby would be wailing her head off, impossible to comfort until she had some food in her tummy.

But today the novelty of Rhys's hard, carved face obviously held an unbreakable fascination for the child as she stared up at him totally absorbed—and totally content.

'So if you'll give her to me, then I'll give her...'

The words died unspoken, shrivelling on her tongue in the face of the fiercely quelling glare he turned on her, reducing her to silence without a word needing to be spoken. He barely lifted his eyes for a second, but it was enough.

'You get the food,' he said with icy precision. 'I'll give it to her.'

'But...'

'I'm going to have to learn, Caitlin.'

It was expressed with a sort of exasperated finality that showed he clearly did not expect her to argue in the least.

'If I'm going to be looking after her in the future, then I need to know what to do.'

Oh, this was getting worse and worse. She couldn't let things go on this way. She just couldn't.

'But...' she repeated.

'But nothing, Caitlin.'

Rhys dismissed her protest with the same casual indifference with which he might flick away an irritating fly.

'Fleur is hungry so she'll need something to eat. And I'll need you to show me what she has so that I can prepare it again later.'

'So that I can prepare it again later.' Even the 'if's had gone now, Caitlin registered with a terrible sense of galloping inevitability. There was no doubt in Rhys's mind that the baby was his and that as his child she was going to be with him in the future. His statement made a fact out of something that wasn't a fact. And she was going to have to tell him so.

Tell him and face the inevitable explosion.

'Rhys, I don't think that's a good idea,' she began cautiously, feeling as if she was treading on eggs, walking blind, feeling her way in desperation. This must be what it felt like edging your way along a mountainous, snow-filled valley where there was a constant threat of terrifying avalanches, never knowing quite when some small stumble, or the slightest careless sound might trigger off disaster. When thousands and thousands of tons of brutally destructive snow would break free and come thundering down, crushing and devastating everything in its path.

'I think it's the obvious idea,' he countered decisively, turning another of those dark-eyed glares on her colourless face. 'It's the only way I'm going to learn.'

'But...'

She'd nerved herself to tell him; had actually opened her mouth to say the words that would bring that avalanche crashing down. But if she managed to make a sound, it was never heard. Instead, it and every other noise in the room was suddenly drowned out by the high, demanding wail that Fleur at last unleashed to display her disapproval.

Whether it was because she had finally realised that she was in fact hungry, or because her new-found favourite had allowed himself to be distracted, turning his attention from the baby to Caitlin in a way she totally disapproved of, Caitlin couldn't guess. All she did know was that, having finally remembered what her vocal chords were to be used for, the little girl simply let rip. Her small head went back, her rosebud mouth opened, her face went bright red, and she yelled. Yelled at the top of her voice her total displeasure at being left alone and disregarded like this.

'I warned you she was hungry!' Caitlin managed, with her own voice carefully pitched above the row. 'I thought she was rather too well-behaved.'

'Well, she certainly isn't now!'

In spite of the tension that still gripped her, the way that her heart was tap-dancing nervously against the sides of her chest, Caitlin still couldn't totally suppress the urge to let a fleeting smile escape. Only for a second though and then she hastily caught it back, not daring to risk Rhys even guessing at what she was thinking.

Now he would see what being a parent was really like! Now he would realise that a six-month-old baby wasn't all sweetness and light—and smiles and coos. Now he would have his nose rubbed in the harsh realities of just how impatient a hungry little one could be. Once Fleur got going, her cries could threaten to pierce eardrums, and she had staying power that was positively exhausting. Rhys was getting a much-needed early lesson in the reality of baby care—with a vengeance.

'Do you want me to take her?'

She was thankful for the way that Fleur's high-pitched screams drowned out the undercurrent of triumph that might otherwise have shown in her voice.

'I said no. If she needs food—you get that.'

Infuriatingly he appeared totally unconcerned. Instead, he walked around the room, somehow sensing intuitively that the movement would soothe the hungry child.

'I really think—' Caitlin tried again, the need to have Fleur back in her care overcoming any thoughts of caution.

'Caitlin, I said I'll look after her. I need to learn.'

'But it would be better if you gave her to me. And much better if we talk about this. You see…'

The words died on her lips in the face of the coldly quelling glance he turned on her.

'No, *you see*,' he stated with dangerous emphasis. 'I have waited three long months to get my child into my arms. And that is where she's staying. Either that or I walk out of here right now…'

It was no empty threat. He meant it. She knew that from the cold burn in his eyes, the fiercely uncompromising tone, and the way he looked towards the door as if he was already out of it.

But even knowing that, she couldn't leave things unsaid. She would have to tell the truth some time.

'But she's not—'

He turned before she completed the first word. The two long, determined strides he took across the room, away from her, had panic clutching at her throat, silencing the rest of her protest. She had no doubt at all that if she hadn't he would have been gone before the next syllable could form.

'All right! I'll say nothing! Just stay—*please* stay.'

The seconds while he reconsidered were some of the longest of her life. If he decided to go she knew she would only have one alternative—to shout the truth after him. And that was the worst possible way to do it. For one thing, she doubted that he would believe a word she said, the mood he was in.

Slowly, agonisingly slowly, Rhys swung on his heel to face her.

'Not another word…'

'Not one. I promise. Just let me feed the baby.'

He had her in a cleft stick, she knew it, and so did Rhys, she admitted to herself as she hurried into the kitchen and started pulling out formula, baby food. The trouble was, she wasn't in exactly the sort of trap that Rhys believed she was in.

But she would keep quiet—for now. It was safer that

way. Perhaps when Fleur was fed and comfortable, when the little girl had settled down for her nap, then they could talk.

And though her stomach quailed queasily at the thought, every nerve knotting tight, she knew that then she would have to tell him.

By the end of the afternoon Rhys felt surprisingly tired, but infinitely satisfied—and supremely happy.

Who would ever have dreamed that one tiny person could be so demanding and so complicated to handle? Feeding her had been fun—the changing of her nappy less so; but the real challenge had come with getting her to sleep. Clearly the upset to her routine, the arrival of someone new in her life, had sparked off an unsettled mood that had turned her from a sweet, contented little honey into an awkward, demanding monster, who had yelled if he held her, yelled if he put her in her cot, yelled if he rocked her…

Or perhaps she just sensed the atmosphere in the small house. It wouldn't take much to do so. Although Caitlin was almost totally silent, only speaking when she had to, you could cut the tension in the room with a knife. And, although polite, every answer she gave was frigid and stiff, cold as ice.

So it was no wonder that the baby had taken so long to settle and drift off to sleep.

And even when she had, he hadn't been able to leave her. Instead, he had stayed, simply standing by the cot, watching her sleep, unable to believe that she was real. Though he knew that it would wake her up again, he was severely tempted to pick her up, cuddle her, feel the soft, delicate warmth of her, smell the sweet, baby scent of her skin, listen to the ridiculous snuffles and chirrups she made as her way of communicating.

But she was asleep now. And, like it or not, he had to

leave her. There were things that he and Caitlin had to talk about. Things they had to thrash out.

And this time he was keeping his head!

All right, admit it, he told himself furiously—the real phrase he needed was that this time he was *thinking* with his head. This time he wasn't going to let his most basic instincts get in the way of the rational thought, the calm approach that was needed.

The problem was Caitlin. Five minutes spent with her and he forgot the control and the experience learned after thirty-two years of living. One look at those eyes, the curves of her body and he reverted to the yearning hunger of an adolescent who had just discovered his sexuality and the attractions of the opposite sex.

And he didn't like the way that made him feel.

This time, he was going to keep his libido firmly under control and discuss things in a cool, calm and above all, damn it, a *controlled* manner.

But first he had to find Caitlin. When he had taken Fleur up to bed she had stayed in the kitchen, but while he was trying to persuade the baby to sleep, he had heard her come upstairs and go into her bedroom.

Not the place he would choose to have the conversation he knew was inevitable. But perhaps if he could persuade her to come downstairs again... Surely this time they could manage to behave like the mature adults they both were and discuss this sensibly.

Calm. Sensible. Rational.

Words that flew straight from his head as soon as he opened the door into the bedroom.

'Caitlin?'

The first thing that hit him was the sight of the bed.

The unmade bed.

The bed on which the covers still lay tangled, the sheets

rumpled, the pillows askew—one of them even lying on the floor where some particularly restless movement had flung it.

Images of the night he had spent in that bed assailed his senses, throwing up memories he both did and did not want to recall. It seemed that the sights and sounds of the night, even the scents—the musky floral of her perfume and her skin—still swirled in the air, making the atmosphere heavy and thick with remembered sensuality.

'What do you want?'

Her voice, cool and unwelcoming, drew his eyes to where she sat on the floor, the curve of her slim hips a provocation in itself. Her brown hair had fallen from the restraining pony-tail, some strands tumbling wantonly across her face, others lingering more sedately within the confines of the elastic band. Her eyes were heavy, the make-up faintly smudged like extra shadows underneath them, and the lipstick she had worn earlier had all but vanished, leaving the soft pink of her mouth completely and sensually natural.

The sweet disorder of her appearance tugged at all the primitive instincts he had sworn to ignore, making him fight to keep his head about the muddying waters of sexuality.

'We need to talk.'

The words fell into a silence in which he knew that they were both thinking of how he had spoken just the same phrase the previous night and she had refused to listen. He could almost see the lines on which her thoughts were running, the same tracks as his were following. The kisses, the touch, the caresses—the journey up the stairs. His body clenched tightly just remembering.

Hell, no!

'We certainly do.'

Her voice sounded blurred, as if it was smudged like her

eyes, making him look closer. Her cheeks seemed to have lost all colour and those brilliant eyes were glistening with more than just their natural brightness.

Tears?

His stomach clenched on another sensation. An even more disturbing one. He moved across the room, sat on the edge of the bed. Near enough, but at the same time far enough away from her.

'What are you doing?'

She shifted her body slightly so that he could see and he cursed silently and savagely inside his head as he realised what she had been doing.

The photograph that he had crushed under his heel still lay on the floor, crumpled and torn. A small waste-paper basket stood beside her and she had been carefully picking up the tiny splinters of glass that lay scattered over the carpet.

Guilt stabbed at him as he remembered the wanton violence with which he had destroyed the photograph. A violence that had come from sheer savage jealousy at the thought that any other man had known her. That she had cared enough to keep the picture of a man who just wasn't worth it.

'What did you say his name was?'

'Josh—Joshua Hewland.'

If his voice had sounded rough, then hers seemed worse. Both of them suddenly seemed to have developed painfully sore throats that made the words scrape over raw vocal cords.

'And you were engaged?'

'I thought we were.'

Her hand crept out, touched the edge of the photograph, then was snatched back again sharply.

'I thought we had an…understanding that we were heading for marriage, even though he'd never actually proposed. But it seemed Josh didn't feel that way. He thought it was just for fun. So he didn't think I would mind too much when he fell head over heels for someone else.'

The opinion Rhys expressed of a man who believed his lover 'wouldn't mind too much' was short, succinct and extremely rude, making Caitlin's mouth twist in wry acknowledgement.

'I might have been able to take that if he'd told me at first,' she said sadly. 'But they had been together for four months before I even found out. She was living in my flat—they—'

'They were carrying on an affair under your roof?' Rhys inserted on a note of disgust when her voice faltered and she looked down sharply, blinking hard against the moisture that flooded her eyes. 'She lived with you?'

Caitlin muttered something that he didn't quite catch and, leaning forward, he put a hand under her chin, lifting her head gently to face him. The tears that glistened over the bronze eyes were for the bastard Joshua, but he felt an unspoken reproach stab at him all the same.

'Where is he now?'

'He—died.'

Oh, hellfire. Rhys's gaze went back to the photograph. To the laughing, handsome face. No wonder she had kept it. No wonder...

'Caitlin, I didn't know. If I had...I'm—'

'No!'

Caitlin had to stop him there.

She had to shut him up. Had to stop him from saying any more. She knew he was going to say he was sorry, and she didn't want that. Anything but that.

Saying he was sorry meant that he was sorry for *every-*

thing. That he was saying once again how much he regretted last night and all that had happened.

How he wished it had never happened.

And she couldn't bear to hear him say those words.

She had come into the room to clear up, ostensibly to pick up the pieces of shattered glass, the splinters of the broken picture frame, but in fact she had just been sitting here, staring at the carpet with eyes that wouldn't focus, lost in her memories.

Memories of last night. And Rhys. And the passion that had flared between them.

And her tears had not been for Josh or the ending of their relationship. Instead they had been for the loss of that wonderful passion, that amazing something that she and Rhys had shared—something she had never known with anyone else.

Something she had hoped might be a beginning.

'No, Rhys, don't! I don't want to talk about it. Any of it. It's past. Done. What we need to talk about is now. The present and what's happening in it.'

'The present,' Rhys echoed. 'That's quite simple. I've got what I came for...'

Fleur.

He had come for Fleur, and now that he had her he was happy. His next words confirmed her fears perfectly.

'I'm going to take her home with me— No?'

She had moved without knowing it. A tiny, automatic shake of her head that, still holding her chin, finger and thumb on either side of her face, he had felt, no matter how small it was.

'I can't go home?' he questioned sharply, his hold on her tightening a notch. 'Why not?'

'Rhys...'

It was all she could say. All she could manage. And after

that her voice deserted her, shrivelling to nothing, no matter how hard she tried to speak.

'Why not, Caitlin?'

Rhys looked deep into the troubled depths of her eyes and suddenly thought he knew what was worrying her. She thought she was going to lose Fleur. Not only that, but she also thought that, like Josh, he was going to turn away from her without a second thought.

Something that made the taut, tense set of every muscle in his face suddenly ease and his stern mouth relax into a smile. Something that made him nod as if in acknowledgement of a secret he felt they shared.

'You don't want me to go? You think that now I have my daughter I'll go—forget you?'

Just for a second his gaze slid away and down, towards the bed on which he sat, its covers still dreadfully disordered after the heated lovemaking of the night.

'Do you think I could forget what we shared? What we had here, together? Caitlin, if I live to be a hundred, I will never forget last night. Passion like that comes into a man's life only once in a blue moon. One night was not enough. It could never be enough.'

It was nothing less than the truth. This woman had got under his skin in a way he had never anticipated. He could never forget her. Hell, he didn't even want to be without her. Right now he had no idea where it might lead, but he knew he wanted to try it.

There was no need for them to fight over this. They could work it together. Himself, Fleur and Caitlin.

'Come with me, Caitlin,' he said with soft urgency. 'Come with me and Fleur.'

His thumb brushed over her cheek, stroking soft patterns on the smooth skin, and his voice wove sweet spells around Caitlin's senses. Spells that whispered of desire and sensuality and an end to loneliness. Promises of time with Rhys.

Promises that tempted her so desperately.

'Come to London with both of us—live with me…'

She couldn't let him go any further.

'No! Never. How can you even suggest that when…I can't…'

'Can't?'

He looked as stunned as if she had just slapped him hard in his face and that stroking thumb stopped moving, tightened cruelly.

'What the hell are you talking about, Caitlin? Of course you can. I have plenty of room—a huge great house that needs a family in it. You want to be with Fleur. What have you to keep you here?'

Nothing. Except that he wouldn't want her—wouldn't want them when he knew. And she had to tell him.

'Everything.'

With a violent effort that tore at her heart she wrenched free of his grip, moving back out of his reach. Clouded amber eyes locked with intent, fixed blue.

'I can't come with you, Rhys.'

'Can't or won't?'

'Can't—won't! I won't come, Rhys—we won't come. I can't let you take Fleur. You can't have her to live with you.'

To her horror he actually laughed. Low and hard, it was a laugh of sheer disbelief. Of total rejection of what she was saying.

'Oh, now I know that you're not seeing straight. You're not talking sense. Of course I can have Fleur to live with me—why do you think I've been searching for her for so long? Why else do you think I came here?'

'No.'

It was a low moan of pain, one that distress forced from her. She had known that this would be hard, but she had never dreamed how hard. How much it would hurt her too.

'Rhys, please, listen to what I'm saying. You can't have Fleur to come and live with you—I can't let you take her. I really can't.'

'I don't think you have any say in the matter.'

If his voice had been dangerous before, then it was positively savage now.

'She's my daughter—my child—mine and Amelie's. I want her and I'm going to have her.'

'But she isn't—that's the whole problem. Oh, Rhys, this is what I've been trying to tell you. You can't have Fleur because she isn't yours. I know what you thought but it just isn't true. Fleur was Amelie's child, yes—but she isn't your daughter.'

CHAPTER NINE

RHYS swung the car around a tight corner and pressed his foot down hard on the accelerator, sending the powerful vehicle hurtling down the road with total disregard for the winding, uneven surface. The brilliant headlights lit up the way in front of him, the trees swaying in the heavy wind, the torrential downpour of rain that sluiced across the tarmac.

The appalling conditions suited his mood. Even the weather seem in harmony with the way he was feeling—though there was nothing at all harmonious about the state of his thoughts. They were a blend of black, blind rage and furious turmoil. And at least the heavy rain meant that there wasn't another car in sight, not another human being on the deserted country roads.

The tyres squealed as he hit another corner. He had no idea where he was or where he was heading. He didn't even know what time it was and quite frankly he didn't give a damn. He just wanted to put as much distance as possible between himself and the source of his black frame of mind.

Caitlin.

Caitlin, the woman he had wanted so much it had driven him halfway insane.

The woman who had stopped him thinking straight, driven him out of his mind. He had to have been out of his head or how had he ended up in this mess?

Caitlin, damn her. Damn her to hell. Caitlin and her lies and her deceit. Caitlin and her burning, golden eyes. Her sexy body, her scented skin.

122

The image of the woman he had shared a bed with the previous night seemed to float before him against the darkened windscreen, threatening to drive him even further into madness.

Caitlin. The woman with whom he had had such an unforgettable night of passion that he knew it would be etched on his brain forever.

Caitlin the unforgettable. Caitlin the gorgeous. Caitlin the temptress. Caitlin the *tormentor*, damn her to hell...

Caitlin...

Caitlin and Fleur.

Another squeal of the tyres, louder than before, marked the way that he had slammed on the brakes, wrenching the car to a brutal standstill.

'Fleur was Amelie's child, yes—but she isn't your daughter.'

Even now, when those words had played over and over inside his head for hours, it seemed, he still couldn't bring himself to actually accept them.

'You're lying!'

That had been his first reaction. The only thing that would come to his mind. The only thing he could force himself to say as he'd jackknifed to his feet, unable to sit there—on that damn bed—any longer.

'You're lying, damn you!'

But, glaring into her eyes, he had had his doubts immediately. She didn't *look* as if she was lying.

'Why would I lie, Rhys?' she had asked and she had actually sounded as if she had had to struggle to get the words out too. As if she regretted having to say them. 'What good would it do me?'

'How the hell should I know?'

But even as he'd thrown the words into her face he'd known. Something of the truth had dawned in his beleaguered brain, forcing its way through the haze of furious rejection.

'You'd get to keep Fleur!' he'd flung at her.

And, seeing her flinch, seeing the rush of darkness into her golden eyes, he'd known that he'd come close to the truth or something like it.

'You never wanted me to have her. You kept her birth—her life—her *existence*—a secret from me!'

'Because Amelie asked me to.'

'While she was alive, I might have understood that. But Amelie is dead! What is it, Caitlin? Are you so desperate for a child of your own that you had to steal mine?'

'She isn't yours!'

He had had to get out then. Get out and give vent to his rage and pain in some way so as to let it out, ease it somehow—anyhow. It was either that or stay there and lash out at what was closest—which in this case would, of course, have been Caitlin. And that would have been so dangerous.

Blinded by the red haze of fury and misery, he had lost his grip on his temper, and on his actions. If he stayed he wouldn't be responsible for what his feelings would drive him to do.

And so he had stormed out, thrown himself into the driving seat of his car, and taken off down the steep, winding drive at a speed that was positively dangerous to life and limb, but which expressed his inner turmoil perfectly.

Which had got him here, wherever here was. By the side of this deserted country road. With the rain lashing down so hard that the windscreen wipers were having to struggle just to cope with it. And with the whirlwind of fury abating but not under control.

He doubted it would ever be under control.

Because he couldn't accept what Caitlin had told him. Wouldn't accept it.

He had given up three, almost four months of his life, devoting them to tracking down and finding the daughter that he had never believed he would have. The baby he had thought would never exist. From the moment he had heard from a mutual friend that Amelie had had a child—and that she had said that the baby was his—he had had only one thought in his head.

To find his child.

Find her and take her home, to live with him. To care for her as a father should, to bring her up in safety and comfort.

And love.

He had fallen in love with the baby even before he had ever met her. And today, when he had held her in his arms for the very first time, he had thought that his heart would burst for the sheer joy and pride of knowing that she was his.

And now Caitlin had taken all that away from him. If she had physically ripped his heart from his chest then it might have hurt less.

If he accepted it.

His fingers drummed restlessly on the rim of the steering wheel as he reviewed the argument he had had with Caitlin. There was something not quite right in there. Something that if he could just remember…

Ma petite Fleur.

It was like a light going on inside the darkened car.

No. He was damn well not giving up.

Edging the car back out onto the rain-washed road, he turned it carefully and set off back in the direction of the hotel, this time at a much less breakneck pace.

When the knock at the door sounded, the last thing Caitlin was expecting was that Rhys would have returned. He had stormed out of the house in such a blinding rage that she fully expected she would never, ever see him again. And so she answered the summons to the door without any hesitation. It was bound to be her father, who, concerned at the way she had never shown up in the main part of the hotel, or contacted him to explain her absence, would want to know how she was.

'I'm sorry, Dad,' she was saying as she pulled open the door to one of the filthiest nights ever. 'You wouldn't believe the sort of day I've had.'

'Oh, I'd believe it all right...'

Rhys didn't wait to be invited in but came straight past her into the hall, bringing with him a flurry of cold night air and a spattering of raindrops on an unseasonable wind.

'I've had much the same sort of time myself.'

'I don't remember asking you to come in!' Caitlin spluttered indignantly, wishing belatedly that she had not opened the door quite so wide and so might have been able to slam it closed before he had intruded with such cold confidence.

'And I don't remember asking you to let me in,' he returned with total indifference. 'I didn't intend to let you say no. Where's Fleur?'

'She's asleep in her cot—it is nearly half-past nine,' Caitlin pointed out. 'I fed her and put her down nearly two hours ago. And don't you dare wake her!' she added as he headed further into the house.

'I've no intention of waking her,' Rhys flung at her. 'What sort of father do you think I am? I take it she should sleep through the night?'

Caitlin noted with a sinking heart and a sense of dread that 'what sort of father'. Clearly, contrary to what she had believed, Rhys had not shaken the dust of the place from his feet and headed for London, ending up miles away from her forever. Instead he had come back in fighting mood.

'Yes, she'll probably not wake till around six in the morning.'

'Good, then that will give us time to talk. And tonight we *are* talking.'

'I certainly wasn't planning on doing anything else!'

'That's good because neither was I.'

Bitter memories of how they had spent the previous night instead of talking made her voice cold and brittle. And the knowledge that she had only herself to blame made things so very much worse.

How she wished that he had turned his back on her and driven off at speed to London. At least then she would have a sort of peace, knowing he would never trouble her again.

Or was she lying to herself—or at least avoiding facing the truth when she told herself that? When she had been feeding and bathing Fleur, trying desperately to divert her thoughts from the moment that she had had to tell Rhys the truth, she had found it impossible to honestly convince herself that she was glad he had gone. The sound of the door slamming behind him had seemed like a darkly ominous sound, marking the end of something that for such a brief time she had had such high and positive hopes for.

High and *foolish* hopes, she had told herself. Impossible, ridiculous, unachievable hopes.

Rhys had not been the sort of man she believed him to be. He had not even been the man she thought he was. Matthew Delaney had never even existed, except in the fantasy of a future she had allowed herself to indulge in for a short, unrealistic time of dreams.

'Do you mind if I go in?'

Rhys's gesture towards the sitting room surprised Caitlin. After the way he had barged into the house, she hadn't expected him to be quite so hesitant about making himself at home.

'Of course not.'

'I'm—' he grimaced in the shadowy hall '—wet.'

'A little damp won't harm. It's not exactly a stately home.'

But when she followed him into the full light of the sitting room her breath caught in her throat as she realised what he meant.

'Wet' was an understatement. He was soaked. The jacket of his suit was patched with great stains of water. The exposed areas of his shirt underneath were sodden and clung to the powerful lines of his chest, in places so transparent that the dark shadow of his body hair showed through the fine material. And his dark hair was black with moisture, flattened to the sides of his head and with streaks of water trickling down his temple and along his forehead so that he swiped at it roughly with an impatient hand, making sure it didn't fall into his eyes.

'What on earth happened to you?'

'It's pouring down outside, in case you hadn't noticed.'

'But you were in your car.'

'At first…'

Rhys's mouth twisted in a wry grimace.

'I set off in my car but then when I came back I realised I wasn't in a calm enough mood to talk about this—not yet. So I went for a walk.'

'In this? Rhys—you idiot!'

'You'd have preferred it if I'd come back here mad as hell and ready to kill?' he enquired with a dry note of mockery.

'As bad as that?'

Caitlin eyed him warily, seeing the flash of still unsubdued anger in his eyes as he nodded.

'As bad as that.'

'Then…'

'No, don't worry,' he put in hastily. 'I've got myself back under control again, I swear. I'll be on my best behaviour from now on—completely civilised.'

'Civilised' and 'under control' were two descriptions that Caitlin couldn't quite equate with Rhys Morgan. At least not with the Rhys Morgan who stood before her. The man she had had dinner with—was it really only last night?— *he* had been supremely civilised and totally controlled. But that man had been the person she thought was Matthew Delaney. And Matthew Delaney was someone who had never existed.

Which was such a tragedy because she had started to feel something very special for him.

'No!'

To her horror, she found that her shock at the path her thoughts had been taking had pushed her into revealing her response quite openly, saying the word out loud. And, hearing it, Rhys drew his dark brows together in a sharp frown.

'No?' he questioned. 'No what? No, I can't stay—or no, you don't believe that I will behave? Because I can assure you I will.'

'Well, that remains to be seen.'

Still shaken by what she had revealed, if only to herself, Caitlin found that she couldn't look at him, couldn't meet the deep blue of those probing eyes. She was too afraid of what she might reveal to him, afraid that he might actually be able to reach into her thoughts and find out what was there.

'You'll need a towel—take your jacket off and put it on the back of a chair while I get you one. A dry shirt would be a good idea too.'

'Caitlin, don't fuss…'

'I'm not *fussing*! I'm being practical.'

And snatching at any possible excuse to keep busy, to move away from him and into the kitchen, where a freshly dried batch of washing had a clean blue towel neatly folded on the top of it.

'Here.'

She tossed it at him from the doorway on her way upstairs. Anything to keep moving, to stop thinking.

But when she came down, the sight that met her eyes through the open door was enough to make her want to go right back upstairs again and stick her head under a cold, hard shower.

Rhys had taken his jacket off as she had suggested and it was hanging neatly over the back of a chair. But he had also taken his shirt off, tossing that onto the settee, and was using the towel to wipe his chest and arms dry, exposing too much toned muscle and lean strength for Caitlin's peace of mind. He'd clearly rubbed at his hair too, absorbing the worst of the rainwater from it, and it lay in wild disorder about his head, giving him an untamed, rakish look that brought back disturbing, unwanted memories of the way he had looked in the middle of the night.

In the middle of the night when her own hands had disordered his hair. When her fingers had clutched at it in the throes of her fulfilment, her body arched tightly under his as they climaxed together.

No, no, no, *no*!

'Here…'

She flung the shirt at him as she had done the towel, but, being of far lighter material, it only floated halfway across the room, falling well short of his reaching arm and landing on the carpet instead.

'Thanks.'

Of course, he had to discard the towel before coming

forward to pick it up. And then for some reason he paused, the faded denim material in his hands, an unreadable expression on his face.

'What's wrong? Won't it fit?'

The whole point had been for him to put it on—fast. The sight of his naked torso, the whipcord strength of his arms, the black hair-hazed chest, the narrow waist was making her heart thud uncomfortably, her breath suddenly uneven and raw.

'Yeah, it should fit.'

Rhys shook out the shirt from its ironed folds, holding it up in front of him, which at least eased her edgy feelings just a little.

'Well, put it on! Just what is wrong?'

'This shirt? It's not *his*?'

'His?'

For several seconds she couldn't even begin to think who he might mean.

'It's my father's, if you must know—is that a problem?'

'No.' Rhys shook his dark head, sending the damp hair flying even more. 'Not at all.'

He was shrugging himself into the shirt when the truth dawned on her.

'You didn't think it was *Joshua's*? You did, didn't you?' she added, interpreting the look he turned on her. 'You actually thought I'd keep his shirts...'

'You kept his photograph.'

'Which you destroyed.'

He actually had the grace to look rather shamefaced at that, but that only made her feel worse about the petty scoring she had indulged in. She had been living in the past and she knew it. She just hadn't had the courage to take the final step forward, into the future.

Rhys had made sure of that. And in another world, in

other circumstances, she might have thanked him for giving her the much-needed push. But not here; not now.

'Have you eaten?'

Once again it was the need to distract herself from her thoughts that made her ask.

'You really are determined to look after me, aren't you?' He was unbuttoning the shirt as he spoke, pushing his arms into the sleeves, shrugging it up to cover his broad shoulders.

'Well, don't read anything into it. It's just that, if I know anything, your mood will be a lot milder if you're not hungry as well as furious. And I need you to be prepared to listen.'

'Oh, I'll listen all right.' Somehow he made it sound like a threat rather than a promise. 'But I'll have plenty to say as well. And no, I haven't eaten—but you don't have to—'

'I can rustle up a sandwich and coffee at least. I could do with something as well.'

Liar! her conscience reproved her. She doubted if she could eat a thing. Her stomach seemed to be turning somersaults that left her feeling queasy and her mouth and throat were so painfully dry that swallowing would be almost impossible.

She should feel better now that he'd pulled on the shirt, but in fact the effect was the exact opposite. The worn and faded cotton clung to the firm lines of his strong frame and the blue denim did amazing things for his eyes. The deep brown hair, drying fast now, still fell in ruffled softness over his wide forehead, and the shirt hung open over the curling hair on his chest.

And he didn't appear to have any intention of fastening it up.

'Do you want any help?'

'No, thank you.'

It came out with a force that was fiercer than she had intended, her struggle to keep her thoughts from wandering off onto paths she didn't want to follow meaning that she didn't quite have full control over her voice.

'I won't be a minute. And then you can tell me whatever it is you want to talk about.'

'You know perfectly well what we have to discuss,' Rhys told her, his stony face matched by the curt, cold words. 'You're going to tell me why you say Fleur isn't my child when I believe I have evidence that she is. And you're also going to say whose child you claim she is. And I warn you, Caitlin, I'll accept nothing but the truth.'

CHAPTER TEN

HE SHOULDN'T be here.

He had made a major mistake in coming back at all, Rhys told himself, and now he very definitely shouldn't be here, in this room that seemed to hold shadows of the previous evening wherever he turned.

To sit on the settee invited memories of sitting there, with Caitlin close by. Of the scent of her skin, the feel of her hand on his, her kiss, the journey to the stairs...

And so he prowled round the room, restless as a caged tiger, wishing himself anywhere but here.

And yet where the hell else could he be?

Only last night he had hunted for some sign, some small clue to his daughter, what she looked like, what sort of personality she had. He had wanted so desperately to see her that he had barely been able to contain himself, and yet here he was now, no more than twenty-four hours later, with everything turned upside-down.

He had seen his daughter—seen *Fleur*, held her, felt her small, warm little body close to his. He had fulfilled that dream, only to have it shattered right there in front of him like the splinters of glass from the photograph frame on the floor upstairs.

'Damn it!'

He slammed a fist down hard onto the back of a chair in a wordless expression of the rage and frustration that was eating away at him inside.

He wanted his child—the child he had thought that

134

Amelie would never give him. He had devoted himself to looking for the baby, only to be told she wasn't his.

'Please leave me some furniture intact.'

Caitlin's tone was cool and controlled as she walked across the room with a tray of cups and plates that she set down on the small dining table.

'I'd prefer it if you didn't take out your bad mood on my belongings.'

Rhys flung a black glare in her direction, hating the feeling of having been caught making such a revealing gesture. He didn't want her to know just how bad he was feeling.

And he would *hate* it if she came anywhere near guessing how much worse she made him feel.

'I thought you said that you had your bad mood under control.'

'I said that I'd behave in a civilised manner—and I will,' Rhys snarled, welcoming the rush of anger that left no room in his mind for the other, more disturbing, more distracting thoughts. 'So long as you play your part.'

'My part being to tell you what you want to know and be quick about it?'

She was pouring coffee as she spoke, concentrating just a little too hard in a way that revealed her thoughts were not on the small practical action. And as they had done on the previous night he could see how her white teeth dug into the softness of her bottom lip, worrying at it sharply.

'Well, don't worry. I don't want you to stay here any longer than you absolutely have to. So I suggest we get this over as quickly as possible.'

'I couldn't agree more.'

If they got this mess sorted out fast then he might just be able to keep a grip on himself and not give in to the stupid impulse to grab her and kiss her senseless. Kiss that prissy, pursed-up look from her luscious mouth. Kiss away the prim, controlled words. Kiss her out of the angry, defensive mood she was in now and into the yearning, sensual surrender that had taken possession of them both the night before.

Kiss her back into his bed.

Kiss them both back into the ecstasy they had discovered together last night.

'So talk…'

He had to give himself a fierce mental shake to get his thoughts back in line, let alone to focus on what he wanted to say. Luckily Caitlin was settling herself in an armchair, taking her mug of coffee with her, and so she didn't seem to register his momentary abstraction, the hungry way his eyes followed her.

'What *do* you want to know?'

'I think you know the answer to that already.'

Rhys made himself take the coffee and, because she had made them and so he felt obliged to show an interest, a sandwich too, before he seated himself in the chair opposite her, leaning back against the cushions and crossing his legs at the ankles.

She looked tired, pale and worn down. The white top that had been so clean and fresh when she had put it on that morning was now considerably worn, obviously after some time spent with Fleur. There was even a small milky stain up high on her left-side shoulder. But Rhys had to admit that, although he had seen many beautiful and supremely elegant women dressed in the most superb selection of designer clothes, none of them had ever been a patch on her for the sheer elemental pull of her feminine sexuality, her total appeal to all that was most deeply male in him.

An appeal he really had to learn to ignore, or she would run rings round him and he would never learn the truth.

'I want you to tell me precisely why you believe Fleur is not my child and—'

'I was told.'

'Who told you? Amelie?'

'No.' Caitlin stared down into the top of her coffee mug, where a creamy circle of foam was whirling frantically in a wild circle, much like the thoughts inside her head. 'Not exactly.'

'And what the hell does "not exactly" mean?'

'It means I—overheard her talking to someone, and what she said seemed to confirm what I'd been told.'

'I repeat,' Rhys stated coldly, 'told by whom?'

'Someone—'

She broke off sharply as Rhys slammed his mug down on the tiled hearth and sat up straight again, abandoning his earlier relaxed position.

'Stop playing games, Caitlin!'

'I'm not!'

The distress in her voice was put there by the thought of how totally different this scene was from the way it had been last night. Then she had curled up on the settee, as close to him as she could possibly get, and the atmosphere had been warm, relaxed—sensual.

This time they were positioned at opposite sides of the fireplace, like long-ago duellists facing each other, sizing each other up, just waiting for the word to fire.

And the feeling in the room couldn't be colder, more hostile if it tried.

'I'm not playing games! This is awkward for me.' And painful.

For a moment she thought he was going to push her, force her to give him details she wasn't yet ready to reveal. Instead he drew in his breath sharply, reached for his mug again, and waited. But this time he didn't relax and instead sat stiffly upright, eyes once more fixed on her face.

'So you overheard Amelie talking to ''someone'' and ''someone'' told you—would these two ''someones'' happen to be the same person?'

Caitlin nodded silently and then, because he was obviously waiting for more, pushed herself to add, 'Fleur's—her father.'

'And he would be?'

It was the question she most dreaded. The one she would have avoided if she could.

She took a deep breath, brought it out slowly and reluctantly.

'Josh.'

She knew he'd heard; knew he'd registered the importance of the name. But still he leaned forward as if to capture an elusive word.

'Say that again.'

'Josh—Joshua Hewland!'

'Your almost-fiancé? Caitlin—I said—'

'I know what you said—and yes, damn you! *Yes!* The man I thought I was going to be engaged to—to marry—'

'He—and Amelie? The woman he betrayed you with was Amelie?'

How many times did she have to spell it out?

'Yes.'

'I see.'

'Do you?'

'Oh, yes, I see all right. I see it all. And I understand so much more, so much that hasn't made any sense—until now. I could never understand why a young single woman, with all of her life ahead of her, should want to tie herself down by taking on the care of another woman's child.'

'I told you! Amelie asked me to!'

'When?'

'It was in the hospital—after the accident—'

'There's something here I don't understand,' Rhys put in sharply. 'I was told that Amelie—that what killed her was the fact that she had a weak heart. But you claim it was a car crash.'

'It was both,' Caitlin told him sombrely. 'It was her heart that caused the crash. She was driving and she had an attack—drove the car right off the road and into a wall. Josh was killed outright. Amelie—well, they thought they could save her because she wasn't badly injured. But then she had another attack...'

'I see.'

'But before that she knew she—she knew. So she said that if anything ever happened to her would I promise to look after Fleur? And of course I said yes.'

'Of course.'

He made it sound as if she had committed some sort of a crime rather than try to help.

'And what does that mean?'

Rhys turned a black look on her, then glanced down at the sandwich in his hand and dropped it back down onto his plate as if he had just discovered that it was dry and stale.

'Well, naturally you would want to take care of the baby once you knew she was your precious *Joshua's* child. The man you were carrying a torch for—'

'Shut up!'

It was low and flat, no emotion in it. She couldn't find the right emotion. Because there was no way she could deny what he was saying. It was true, some of it at least.

She had wanted Fleur because the little girl had been part of Josh. Something real and warm and living that she could hold on to and into whom she could pour all the love that Josh hadn't wanted. With Fleur she hadn't felt quite so lost and alone. She had had Josh's child, as she had always dreamed of having, even if she wasn't actually the baby's mother.

At least that was how it had been at the beginning.

But very soon she had come to love Fleur for herself. The little girl was part of her life. It would kill her to let the baby go now.

'What's wrong, Caitlin?' Rhys taunted. 'Can't you take the truth? Can't you face the facts? You lost your precious Josh to Amelie—and now you want—'

'I said shut up!'

Caitlin pushed herself to her feet, facing him furiously, golden eyes blazing defiance.

'You want to be careful, you know, Rhys. You don't want to start flinging round words like *facts* and the *truth*! Not when you're on such shaky ground there!'

Her outburst took him aback, leaching the colour from his face so that there were white marks etched around his mouth and his eyes seemed impossibly dark and shadowed.

'Oh, yeah?' he managed but his voice had lost much of its earlier bite.

'Yes!'

Realising she was waving her coffee mug in the air like a dangerous weapon, Caitlin whirled away to dump it back on the tray, heedless of the way that the deep brown liquid slopped over the sides, soaking into one of the abandoned sandwiches.

'And what do you mean by that?'

'You know what I mean!'

Coming round the table, Caitlin rested her hands on the polished wood, leaning forward to emphasise the point she was trying to make.

'You're the one who won't accept the truth when it's

handed to you on a plate! I've told you that Fleur isn't yours but you won't believe it. You won't—'

'I can't,' Rhys inserted suddenly, stopping her dead. 'I *can't*,' he repeated when she could only stare at him, too stunned to speak, too stunned to think.

She didn't want to understand. She most definitely didn't want to sympathise—but she found that that was just what she was doing. She would have thought that it was impossible for Rhys to lose any more colour, for the skin on his face to draw any tauter, be stretched any further over the broad lines of his cheekbones. At his jaw a single muscle jerked as if in protest at the pressure of being held so tight. And his eyes seemed to be all black, no trace of blue even at the most outer edge of the iris.

'I can't believe it,' he said again.

'But—but you have to.'

He was silent for so long that she thought he had actually lost his voice. Either that or he had finally accepted the truth but couldn't bring himself to say so.

But then he moved, setting his mug and plate down on the hearth and getting to his feet with a strange, uncharacteristic slowness. To Caitlin's shocked eyes, it was almost as if he had aged ten years or more in the space of the ten stunned seconds that had ticked away so ominously.

'I can't accept it,' he repeated. 'And I won't—and before you say it again, no, I don't have to accept it either. You see, I know something that you don't know.'

Behind him, the clock on the mantelpiece began to strike the hour, making Caitlin almost jump out of her skin. The slow, sonorous strokes seemed unnaturally loud in the cold, brittle silence that had suddenly engulfed them. Too loud for her to talk against.

Instead she waited, not thinking, barely breathing, concentrating solely on counting from one to ten inside her head.

…eight, nine, ten…

And still the silence dragged on because now she didn't know how to break it. She had no idea what to say. Except for the one obvious question. The one she didn't dare to ask.

'What's wrong, Caitlin?' Rhys asked finally, just at the moment that the silence threatened to stretch her nerves to breaking point and still she couldn't find the words to ask. 'Lost for words? Or perhaps this time *you're* the one who can't face the truth. The one who doesn't want to know.'

'I—no—I…'

Her voice failed her, croaking embarrassingly, and she had to stop, swallow hard, before she could try again.

'I don't believe you,' she managed unevenly. 'There isn't anything—there can't be anything.'

The arrogance of his cool, unrelenting stare, the way one black eyebrow rose in cynical questioning, almost destroyed her.

'All right!' she burst out. 'All right, damn you! What is it? What have I missed? What is it you claim to know?'

And strangely now, for some reason, Rhys actually appeared to hesitate. He looked deep into her face, then down at the floor, traced the shape of a flower in the carpet with the toe of his boot, drew in his breath on a long, slow sigh. Then he let it out again in a rush as he pushed both hands through his hair, flexing his shoulders in a shatteringly uneasy gesture.

'You first,' he said.

'That's not f—' Caitlin began but he cut her off with a dismissive wave of his hand.

'I don't give a damn about what's fair! Nothing in this whole bloody mess is *fair*! So let's not waste time on that. You tell me why you believe Joshua Hewland is Fleur's father.'

CHAPTER ELEVEN

SHE didn't dare to argue. It would be wasted energy; she knew that. And besides, like Rhys, she wanted this sorted—if it was at all possible to get it sorted.

'He told me.'

'Hewland? Not Amelie?'

'No...'

She felt as uncertain as she sounded. When Josh had told her, she could see no reason to doubt him. But now...

'When and why?'

'Why did he tell me?'

Caitlin dug sharp teeth into her bottom lip, using the small physical pain to try and distract her from the memory of the much more intense emotional one.

'Because I'd found out about him and Amelie. Because I'd challenged him with my suspicions that he was being unfaithful. And because he'd wanted to prove how committed to her he was.'

'By saying they were having a child together?'

Was that a note of sympathy in his voice? Caitlin couldn't bear even to consider that it might be. She didn't want Rhys's sympathy—his pity. Right now, it felt so much worse, so much more painful than ever Josh's betrayal had done.

To her horror, bitter tears stung the back of her throat so that she could only nod silently.

'And that was the only time?'

She wished it was.

'No; later—when it was all out in the open about him

and Amelie—he kept making comments, saying things like ''If I'm going to be a dad.'' And Amelie never contradicted him.'

'Tell me something.'

Rhys's tone had sharpened noticeably so that Caitlin was reminded irresistibly of the cross-questioning scene in a courtroom drama she had recently watched on television.

'Your…this Joshua—was he rich, by any chance?'

'Loaded.'

Caitlin's mouth twisted as she said it.

'His family own a string of hotels—a major concern, not like this little place. That's how we met. I worked…'

The words trailed off as she saw his expression, recognised the way his thoughts were heading.

'You think Amelie…?'

'I *know* Amelie—knew her,' he corrected awkwardly. 'She always had an eye for the main chance where money was concerned. If she had thought that Hewland could keep her in the manner to which she'd once become accustomed, then I'm afraid she wouldn't have let a small thing like his possible engagement to you stand in the way.'

'You think she…'

It was just a whisper, and her hand crept up to her mouth as if to stop the words she didn't want to hear escaping.

Rhys nodded sombrely.

'If you're asking if I think she deliberately targeted Joshua—set herself at him, in spite of knowing how you felt about him—then the answer's yes. I can well believe that's exactly what she did. I learned that to my cost when I found out why she'd married me. She was an actress, but she hadn't had any decent parts in almost two years. She had no money of her own—and I was a blind, besotted fool who had plenty.'

'So why did she leave you?'

'She knew I wanted kids. She didn't—or so she said. So she walked out. She stayed away until she ran out of money and then she came crawling back, claiming she wanted a reconciliation. I swallowed that story just long enough to let her back into my bed, but when she made it plain that all she wanted was my money I told her to get out.'

'So she came to France. Where I met her and invited her to come and stay for a while. And within a week she was sleeping with Josh.'

Caitlin shook her head, her bronze eyes wide and dazedly unfocused in shock and disbelief.

'I'm sorry.'

Rhys had to say it. She looked so emotionally battered— so pale and vulnerable—that no one with an ounce of human feeling could have felt anything but sympathy for her right at this moment. Silently he cursed Amelie, who, with characteristic carelessness for other people's feelings, had walked into this woman's life and totally destroyed it. And there was a nasty twist of guilt in there too at the thought that if he had had more patience with Amelie—or at least provided her with the income she wanted—then his wife would never have set herself at Josh, stealing him from Caitlin so cold-bloodedly.

Though if the truth were told, Caitlin hadn't lost much when Joshua Hewland had transferred his affections from her to Amelie. If he could be that easily seduced, then he was not truly husband material.

As he'd expected, his sympathy had the effect of toughening Caitlin's state of mind. Her chin came up defiantly and her eyes clashed sharply with his.

'But this doesn't prove anything about Fleur. I overheard Amelie saying that Josh *could* be the father.'

'But not that he *was*. What name did Amelie put on the birth certificate?'

He knew that she was following his line of thought when he saw how her face changed, the look in her eyes.

'She—she didn't. She left the name off completely.'

'And don't you think she *would* have put it in there if she could? If she could have proved to Josh—and his family—that the baby was his? Don't you think she'd have asked them to take care of Fleur if it was true?'

'So she conned Josh too.'

He hated the tears that flooded her eyes. Hated the fact that they were there for Josh—that even after the way the bastard had betrayed her she could still weep for him. But all the same he couldn't stop himself from moving to her side, taking her in his arms, holding her tight.

Too tight for his own peace of mind.

He didn't want to feel the sudden jolt of his heart, the instant tightening of his body. He didn't want to sense his blood heat in his veins, his pulse speed up, the basic, primal yearning uncoil deep in the pit of his stomach. But he couldn't stop himself.

One breath of the scent of her skin, the perfume of her hair as he came so close, one touch of his skin on hers, as his hand fastened over her bare arm in the short-sleeved top, and he was lost. The need to kiss her, caress her, to *take* her, make her his and his alone, swept over him like a tidal wave, drowning him instantly, even as he struggled to resist it.

But he *had* to resist it. At least for now, until they had this whole damn mess sorted out.

If they ever could get it sorted out.

Against his shoulder he felt Caitlin stir and sigh, drawing in her breath on a faint sound that was almost a sob.

'There was something you said. Something about—something you knew that I didn't…'

'Her name.'

'What?'

Tilting her head up, she looked into his face, a faint, puzzled frown drawing her brows together.

'The baby's name—Fleur. It was what I—once—used to call Amelie.'

The memory was bitter, but overlaying it was the softer, sweeter one of the moment he had held the little girl—his little girl, he was sure—in his arms for the first time.

'*Ma petite fleur,*' Caitlin said, obviously remembering. 'My little flower.'

'Yes. That's it. So you see, if she used that name for the baby, then it was clearly me she was thinking of. Naming her baby for its father. For something I said.'

She was silent so long that he thought she would never answer. But then at last she stirred and moved away slightly so that she could look him in the face.

'Oh, Rhys—I don't know. I don't know what to think. What to do.'

He almost laughed. To him there was no problem. None at all.

He wanted his child. And he wanted this woman. If he had any doubts, then coming back here tonight had wiped them from his mind. Holding her as he had been just a few moments ago, he had known that he would do anything, anything at all, if he could just keep her with him, get her back into his bed.

Keep her in his life.

'That's easy,' he said lightly.

No need to show her yet how much this meant to him. No need to come on heavy and intense when she obviously wasn't ready for it. She had had enough to cope with today already. The revelations about Fleur, about Amelie, and of course about her beloved Joshua had been hard enough for her to take. He didn't want to overload her with anything more.

'Easy?'

'Of course. I've said it before. I've told you what we do.'

She looked strangely dazed, unbelieving.

'You said it before—you mean when you told me I could come and live with you?'

It wasn't the reaction he'd expected. It wasn't anything like the response he'd thought she might have. OK, so he hadn't been fool enough to think that she would fall into his arms straight away. That she'd be overwhelmed with delight at the prospect of moving to London, of starting life afresh in the capital.

But he had expected that she would at least be moderately pleased—at worst accepting of the idea.

Instead she looked as if he'd just suggested that she sell herself—and the baby—to the nearest white-slave trader.

'Why would you think that would work?'

'I would have thought that was self-evident—I've made no secret of the fact that I want you. And you're plainly not…averse to me. Oh, come on, Caitlin!'

His exasperation began to show through, his control over his voice slipping as she still looked dubious.

'It's the obvious answer.'

'It isn't to me.'

'And can you come up with another one that means I get Fleur but you don't have to—?'

'You get Fleur!'

Caitlin had been struggling with her temper. She had been fighting a losing battle with the words of shock and disappointment that had been forcing themselves up her throat, threatening to spill out, pour themselves in a tirade of pain and distress at the thought of what he was offering. And now she gave up.

Twisting away from him, she whirled to face him fully, eyes blazing rejection, hands clenched into fists at her sides.

She couldn't hold back any longer. Couldn't hide her unhappiness at the realisation that he only saw her as a way to get Fleur. That she was part of a package deal, along with the baby he believed was his daughter.

The baby who was truly the one he wanted. While she was just an added extra. A live-in nanny for the baby, who was also someone he fancied sleeping with on the side. A nice sexual bonus, one that also got rid of the potential problems she could cause if she decided to fight him for the baby.

'You get Fleur!' she repeated, her voice creeping up an octave or more in her distress. 'And Fleur's what you really want!'

'Caitlin...'

There was an ominous note in his voice now. One that warned of the dangers of the path she was following, threatened retribution if she didn't see sense.

Sense as he saw it.

'Stop this stupidity, Caitlin! Of course I want Fleur. I've always wanted her, ever since I learned she existed. I want to take her home, to live with me, grow up to know me. She's my baby—my child—'

'There isn't any proof of that!'

She regretted the words as soon as she had said them. There wasn't any proof that Fleur *wasn't* Rhys's child either. There was no proof either way.

'Oh, so that's it!'

'That's what?' she managed miserably, knowing deep down inside that really she didn't have to ask.

She knew from his face, from the way that his eyes had

turned to the icy blue of an Arctic sea, the hard set to his jaw, the cruel, bitter line to his mouth, just what was in his mind. There was only one interpretation he would have put on her reaction. And she knew without a hope of redemption just what that was.

His thoughts had gone immediately to Josh. To his firmly held belief that she was still in love with the man who she had once believed was going to be her fiancé—her husband. He still thought that she couldn't get over his death.

And his first words in response confirmed as much.

'It's him, isn't it—it's Hewland?'

He spat the name out as if it was a curse that tasted vile in his mouth.

'You still can't let go of Joshua Hewland. You're still carrying a torch for the bastard, even after the way he treated you.'

She shook her head, but her eyes wouldn't meet his, and she knew that Rhys would interpret that as meaning that she wasn't telling the truth. That she was avoiding his gaze because she couldn't admit that he was right.

But at least letting him think that was safer than letting him guess at the real truth.

A truth that she was only just beginning to realise for herself.

That she was in love with Rhys. That once again she had been foolish enough, naïve enough, to give her heart to a man who really didn't care for her at all. A man who just wanted to use her to get what he wanted—Fleur.

'I don't believe it!'

'Believe what you like!' It was the nearest she dared to come to defiance and she knew the danger she had provoked as soon as she saw the darkening of his eyes.

'At least Josh wanted me for myself—for a while; he

didn't just want me as part of a job lot with a baby. At least Josh, whatever his faults, spared me that.'

'So you're still obsessed with him.'

It was a vicious snarl, one that made her blood run cold just to hear it.

'The bastard can still reach out from beyond the grave and hold you captive. Well, let's see…'

She didn't see the movement coming, wasn't prepared for the way that he suddenly pounced, so when his hand came out and fastened on her arm she wasn't prepared, had no defences available, no way of fighting him.

Before she quite realised what was happening he had twisted her violently into his grip, his arms coming tight round her, hauling her up against the hard length of his body.

'Well, let's see, shall we, angel? Let's see, my sweet Caitlin, how your dear, dead Joshua can compare with the touch of a real live, warm-blooded man. Can he hold you like this?'

Deliberately he tightened his grip until the air was crushed from her body, making her gasp in shock and instinctive response.

'Can he touch you, caress you…?'

He suited action to the words, combing long fingers through her hair, stroking his hand all the way down her body.

He curved warm palms over her breasts, squeezed gently until she moaned. And then he took her mouth again, tormenting, teasing, enticing, stroking her tongue with his until her blood caught fire.

'Can he kiss you until you're moaning under his caress? Can he arouse you, wake that yearning sensuality that I know is inside you just waiting for a light to be put to its fuse?'

Once again, he suited action to the words, sliding his hands under the white top, smoothing them over her skin, tracing hot, erotic patterns up to her breasts. He teased her nipples into hungry tightness, tugging at them softly, before his fingers slid under the lacy cups of her bra.

She was weakening. He was winning. He was getting to her; making her melt, making her respond. She couldn't stop herself, couldn't help herself...

'No! No, no, no, *no*!'

With a terrible effort she pulled herself away, the force of the movement throwing her halfway across the room so that she collided painfully with the side of the settee, almost tumbling over onto the striped cushions with the force of the impact.

'Get out!'

She couldn't recognise her own voice in the hard, cold, shrill sound that echoed through the quiet room.

'Get out and stay out! I never want to see you again.'

'What's wrong, sweetheart?' he taunted. 'Can't you cope with a real man? Is that the truth of it—that you can only handle the cold memory of your precious Joshua, not with the red-blooded, passionate feelings of a real man?'

'I can cope with a man but not an animal! And I can handle the *feelings* too—when there are any feelings to handle. But there's only one thing you're after—and I wouldn't honour that with the description of a *feeling*. It's just sex—just lust—nothing more. Now get out. And don't think about taking Fleur with you because if you do then I'll have the police after you as fast as you can blink.'

'And when I claim that she's mine?'

'*Prove it!*'

The words fell into a sudden deep and deadly silence. A silence in which she felt the echoes of her words reverberate around her like the ripples in a pool when a stone was thrown into the water.

'Prove it,' Rhys echoed, injecting the words with deadly venom. 'Oh, I'll prove it all right. I wasn't going to insist on this but you've left me no alternative. I want my child, and no one is going to stand in my way. And Fleur *is* my child—a DNA test should soon prove that incontrovertibly. You'd better hold yourself ready for that, my darling. Because one way or another I'm going to get the evidence that will prove my claim.'

CHAPTER TWELVE

THE letter had been lying on his desk for so long that Rhys had just about forgotten exactly when it had arrived in his office.

It had been there long enough for his secretary to notice and comment more than once about the fact that it was still unopened.

'Is it something you want me to deal with?' she'd asked and had got an unexpectedly short, sharp, and strongly negative response to her question.

'I'm sorry, Ms Scamans,' he'd amended hastily when she'd been plainly indignant. 'It's a personal matter. Something I have to deal with myself.'

Something he *wasn't* dealing with himself, he admitted privately.

Face facts, man! You've been avoiding opening the damn thing for over a week now.

And would go on avoiding it until he could find some way out of his quandary.

Because the truth was that he couldn't think of a way of looking at the question of just who was Fleur's father without the facts creating a whole new set of problems. Ones that now appeared to be worse than the original enquiry that had set him out on this quest in the first place.

If he was Fleur's father, then Caitlin would feel obliged to hand the little girl over to him. He would take her home to live with him—and he would lose Caitlin as a result.

If he was *not* Fleur's father, then Caitlin would keep the

baby and care for her, bring her up as her daughter. And he would have no place in their lives at all.

And no excuse ever to see Caitlin again.

So it seemed that either way he lost.

Lost what really mattered to him—which was the chance of a future with both Fleur and Caitlin in it.

'And why would only having Fleur feel like you've lost?' his personal assistant, Sarah, had asked him one day when, grouchy as a bear with a sore head, he'd growled at her that he'd made a total mess of things, and a fool of himself into the bargain.

'It just would.'

'But I thought Fleur was the one thing you wanted. The only reason you went up there in the first place.'

'She was, but—things changed.'

'Changed how? You met Caitlin?'

'Yes.'

'And? Oh, I see!' she said knowingly when he turned a furious glare on her. 'And now just Fleur is not enough?'

'She's my daughter, Sarah!'

'I know. And this…' Sarah smoothed a caressing hand over the faint swell where her pregnancy was beginning to show '…is my child. Someone I already love to pieces even though we've not yet met. But Damon…' Her face softened and her smile grew as she thought of the tall, dark Greek she was married to. 'Damon's my soul mate. The other half of me. The bit that makes me complete. Without him I would always feel there was something missing.'

'But you love Damon.'

'I know. And what does that tell you about your Caitlin?'

'Are you trying to claim that I'm in love with her?'

'I wouldn't dare!'

Sarah flashed him a teasing smile as she turned and headed for the door.

'But I think you should know that the man I used know as Rhys Morgan went off in pursuit of his daughter—and a very different guy came back.'

A very different guy came back.

Sarah's words echoed in his head now, along with his own thoughts of just a few moments before.

No excuse ever to see Caitlin again.

Did he want an excuse to see Caitlin?

Hell, yes! Any excuse!

In the four weeks since he'd been at the Linford, he'd seen her only on a couple of occasions and each of those had been too brief and too uncomfortable to satisfy the longing he had just to spend time with her. How could they be anything else when he had put his foot well and truly in it by implementing his threat to arrange a DNA test? At least one of those meetings had been when Caitlin had had to take Fleur to a doctor to arrange for the necessary samples to be taken.

Which, of course, had not exactly created a situation that was conducive to anything other than the most constrained and distant conversation.

They had talked about Fleur and how she was sleeping. The fact that she now had a single tooth in her gaping, smiling mouth. That she was putting on weight, growing well...

Everything other than anything important.

And he had sat in that damn doctor's waiting room and longed to kiss her. Longed to take her in his arms and tell her that he had never meant any of it. That he would never take Fleur away from her—that what he wanted was them *both* in his life. For the rest of his life.

And Caitlin had treated him like the enemy that she clearly believed he was. She had held herself stiffly, well away from him. Answered his questions with monosyllables. Turned on him a glare so furious that it should have shrivelled him into a pile of ashes where he sat when Fleur had roared a desperate protest at the doctor's treatment.

And then Caitlin had said goodbye very coldly. And no thank you, she didn't need a lift in his car, in spite of the fact that she blatantly obviously needed a lift in his car, when it was once again pouring with rain and the pushchair meant that she couldn't manage an umbrella as well.

And she had walked away from him without ever looking back.

No excuse ever to see Caitlin again.

Rhys's fingers drummed out a tattoo of impatience on the surface of his desk, the sound becoming softer as they moved over the thick, expensive vellum of the envelope that contained the report that could change his future forever.

No excuse ever to see Caitlin again.

Hell and damnation, he had the perfect excuse to see her right here!

Grabbing the envelope, he pushed it into the inside pocket of his jacket in the same moment as he pressed the switch on the intercom through to his secretary's desk.

'Ms Scamans—cancel everything in my diary for the next week at least. I'm going out of town and I don't expect to be back for some time.'

Caitlin pushed the last of Fleur's little dresses into the suitcase and closed the lid, zipping it firmly to fasten it.

There. She was done.

Lugging the case to the bottom of the stairs, she left it standing in the hall near to the door and went back up to the bedroom to start getting Fleur ready. The little girl was lying happily in her cot, small hands reaching up to pat and pull at the brightly coloured activity toy hanging above her.

'Just a couple more minutes, sweetie.'

They were in good time, Caitlin told herself. And Fleur looked so contented. She could afford to let the little girl have a bit more time.

And she could do with a sit-down.

Thankfully she sank down onto a nearby chair and drew in a couple of deep, slow breaths. She hadn't been feeling too good for the past couple of days and today she had felt rough from the moment she had woken up.

Stress, she had decided, admitting that she had never really fully relaxed since the day she had found out just who Rhys Morgan was. And, with the threat of the DNA test results hanging over her head, she had found it totally impossible to find any real peace of mind. Any day now, Rhys might turn up with a document that proved he really was Fleur's biological father and demand that she hand over his daughter to him.

And besides, she really didn't feel right about keeping the little girl from him any more. She knew that Rhys loved Fleur—she'd seen it happen right before her eyes. Fleur had taken to him with a similar heart-stopping speed. And really, as he and Amelie had still been married when the baby was born, he had every right to make a claim to be her father.

If only she felt well enough to tackle the problem properly. Her energy seemed to have totally deserted her and her stomach had been queasy and nauseous all morning. And that had brought with it worries that she didn't want to consider. Worries that had her counting up dates and getting a result that even stress would not explain.

A sudden shriek of protest from Fleur alerted her to the fact that a small blue rabbit, the baby's favourite toy, had fallen through the bars of the cot and onto the floor.

'Oh, you've lost Flopsy! We can't have that, can we?'

Reacting automatically, she bent down to scoop up the small soft toy, then reeled as the simple action of raising her head again made her thoughts swim, and her stomach heave protestingly.

'Oh, help!'

Tossing the toy back into the cot, she held on to the side of the little bed, struggling to breathe normally, and waiting for the moment to pass.

It didn't. If anything, it got worse.

It was like being on the deck of a rolling and pitching ship, but with the movement being only in her head, not actually underfoot. Her head spun, her stomach lurched, she tasted something bitter in the back of her throat.

'No...'

Scrambling to her feet, she headed desperately for the bathroom, only just reaching it in time. She hadn't eaten much yesterday, even less for breakfast, but her stomach didn't seem to know that, and she ended up in the most ungainly position possible, kneeling over the toilet, retching miserably.

And it was then that she heard the ring at the doorbell.

'Go away!' she groaned.

But then, on second thoughts, maybe it was her father... Lifting her head, she tried to call.

'Dad!'

No, that only made matters worse.

And it couldn't be her father. There was no way he would press the bell that hard, for that long. By now he would have opened the door.

Groaning, she gave in to another attack of nausea. And as she did so she heard the handle being turned, the door pushed open.

Oh, thank heaven!

'Dad!'

'Caitlin? Where are you?'

'Up here!'

Heavy footsteps sounded on the stairs, taking them in leaps of two or more at a time just in the same seconds that she registered that the voice she had heard had most definitely *not* been her father's.

'Oh, no—please, no!'

Could fate really be that cruel? Couldn't the new arrival possibly have been someone—*anyone*—else? Did she really have to face Rhys now, like this, when she felt terrible and must look much, much worse?

But fate was not feeling kind and the bathroom door opened abruptly to admit a tall, dark, masculine figure that looked taller, darker and infinitely more male from her humiliatingly undignified position on the floor.

'Caitlin? The door wasn't locked and I—'

'Go away!'

At least that was what she wanted to say, but the fear of being sick again if she opened her mouth properly made the words come out more like 'Mmph mweay'.

But Rhys ignored them anyway, taking in the situation in a glance and coming down beside her on the floor.

'What's wrong?'

'Isn't it obvious? I'm sick...' she flung at him, only to pay for the foolhardiness of the feeble attempt at defiance by proving her point with a violence and ferocity that left her shivering and exhausted by the time it was over.

'OK, sweetheart, I'm here.'

She had forgotten about Rhys's unwanted presence until she felt the cool hand on her hot forehead, smoothing her hair back from her face. At a welcome pause in the horrible retching, he picked up a clean face cloth, wrung it out in warm water from the tap and then gently wiped her face and mouth with it, smoothing away the mess and the bitter tears at the same time.

And it felt so good, so wonderful, that Caitlin forgot who he was and the threat he had held over her and Fleur, and simply relaxed back into his care, sighing in weak contentment.

There was a long silence, a silence Caitlin wished could go on forever and never break. But she had to face him at some point, and so she wearily forced open her eyes.

'I'm OK now.'

'I doubt that very much,' he returned drily. 'You don't throw up what looks like half the contents of your stomach without there being something very badly wrong.'

'I—think I've stopped being sick. For now at least.'

'Then we'll get you into bed.'

But that was more than Caitlin could cope with. The thought of being helped to bed by this man, of being taken to her bedroom, maybe even undressed coldly and clinically by the same man who had performed those actions with such passion only a few short weeks ago was too humiliating even to think of.

She couldn't let him.

'Oh, no!'

'Oh, yes,' Rhys corrected firmly. 'You clearly aren't fit to manage on your own. And then I'll get the doctor. Where's Fleur?'

'In her cot—she's quite safe…'

The sensation of being on a rolling ship was slowly receding. She was beginning to feel slightly less nauseous, though miserably weak and light-headed.

'And I don't need a doctor…'

A doctor would mean that Rhys would be likely to stick around, at least until the consultation was over. And what a doctor might have to say was something that panicked her even more.

'Really, there's no need…'

She found herself being totally ignored as he helped her to her feet and supported her out of the bathroom and down the landing to the bedroom. It was humiliating to admit, even to herself, how thankful she was for the strength of his arm around her waist, the warm weight of muscle that was holding her up.

'Fleur…' she managed when, feeling slightly breathless and rather more faint than she wanted to acknowledge, she reached her room and was lowered carefully to sit on the edge of the bed.

'I'll check on her. Now, can you get yourself into bed or—?'

'I'll manage!' Caitlin said hastily.

She would, if it killed her. Being undressed by Rhys, looking and feeling as she did now, would be the ultimate embarrassment.

'Well, if you're sure, then I'll look in on Fleur and phone the doctor.'

'There's no need…' Caitlin tried again but she was talking to empty air. Rhys had taken her at her word and was already heading back down the landing to the baby's tiny room.

It was as much as she could do to pull off her jeans and blue T-shirt and crawl under the covers. Finding and putting on a nightdress was just beyond her. With an exhausted sigh of relief she lay back against the softness of the pillows and closed her eyes, willing the room to stop spinning.

She must have drifted off to sleep because the next time she became aware of anything was when Rhys came back into the room, bringing with him the calm, smiling woman who was the local doctor.

But all the calm and the smiles in the world couldn't prepare Caitlin for the results of the examination. The diagnosis that turned her fearful suspicions to terrible reality.

CHAPTER THIRTEEN

'I CAN'T be pregnant! I just can't!'

But Dr Collins was not to be swayed. She simply smiled some more, and patted Caitlin's hand in her calm and reassuring way.

'I think you'll find you can, my dear. I know it's obviously come as a shock to you right now, but once you've adjusted to the idea I'm sure you'll be thrilled. And after all, it's not as if you'll be on your own to cope with this. From what I've seen of your young man, if the way he's been dealing with your little girl is anything to go by, he'll be a wonderful help when the new little one arrives.'

By the time Caitlin had recovered from hearing Rhys described as her 'young man' the doctor had gone and could be heard chatting to the 'young man' himself in the hall as she said goodbye.

And now she had to face Rhys, knowing that he'd been told the news.

Caitlin's insides felt as if someone was tap-dancing all over them while her nerves tied themselves into tight, painful knots that twisted harder and harder with each repetition of the word *pregnant* inside her mind.

Pregnant.

With *Rhys's* child.

Under the cover of the bedclothes her hand crept over the softness of her stomach, still totally flat and showing no sign at all of the momentous event that had happened. In spite of herself her expression softened and she found herself imagining the small baby that was already forming inside her.

Rhys's child. Her child. *Their* child.

'I brought you some dry toast because the doctor said that might help with the sickness.'

Rhys's voice sounded from the door, coolly cynical and slashing into the brief, happy dream she had allowed herself.

'So it seems that we're going to be parents.'

Caitlin's eyes flew open to clash with Rhys's cold, assessing blue stare, and she felt all the wonder and contentment seep away from her like air from a punctured tyre. That had been the dream. This was the reality.

She was going to have a baby with Rhys. With the man who, she was now forced to admit if only to herself, had stolen her heart and offered her nothing in return. A man who had slept with her on the night they had made that baby purely for the most selfish reasons, because he wanted to leave her vulnerable to him so that he could get his hands on Fleur. Well, she was vulnerable to him now all right. As vulnerable as she could possibly be.

And, knowing how Rhys had fought to get custody of Fleur, she could have little doubt that he would come after this baby in the same way.

'She told you, then?'

'She asked if I was the "daddy,"' Rhys returned, still in that bleakly cynical tone.

'And you said…?'

'What do you think I said? I said yes, of course—because I *am*, aren't I?'

He looked at her sharply, blue eyes probing the pallor of her face.

'I *am* the daddy, aren't I?'

In a fury of indignation, Caitlin picked up a piece of

toast and flung it at him, feeling a rush of satisfaction when it hit him squarely on the chest, leaving brown speckled crumbs all over his pale blue shirt.

'Of course you damn well are. Who else could be? I don't exactly making a habit of sleeping with strange men the first night I go out with them.'

'But in my case you made an exception?'

It was openly taunting, something she had to struggle to ignore.

'You didn't go for the morning-after pill, then?'

'If you remember, the "morning after" was interrupted by Mandy bringing Fleur round to my house. And then other things intervened...'

She knew from the look on his face that he was recalling how those 'other things' had included the way she had been forced to tell him that she believed Fleur was not his child.

'After that, neither of us was thinking too clearly.'

'Well, I'm thinking pretty damn clearly now—and what I'm wondering is were you ever going to tell me? If I hadn't turned up here today, would you have let me know?'

'I've barely had time to realise it for myself, let alone decide what I'm going to do.'

'Not I,' Rhys corrected sternly. 'We.'

'We?'

The implications of that single syllable had Caitlin leaning weakly back against the pillows in a moment of total shock.

'What do you mean, we?'

'Oh, come on, Caitlin!' Rhys scorned. 'You are not that ill—or that stupid! You know perfectly well what I mean. It takes two to tango—or, in this case, to make a baby. And, as I was intimately involved in this start of this, then I'm going to stay around to the bitter end.'

'Bitter end' made her wince and despairing tears sting her eyes. It had a terribly dark, cynical sound to it.

'I don't think there's any need for that—'

'And I think there's every need for it, sweet Caitlin. This at least is a baby I *know* is mine! You might wish that it were the child of your unforgettable lover Joshua, but I'm afraid that, unless you believe that he somehow resurrected himself in order to get you pregnant, the blame all lies with me. And I'm staking my claim loud and clear right from the start. There isn't any way I'm letting this child be taken away from me.'

'I—I'll let you see—' Caitlin began, but he cut her off, shaking his dark head adamantly as he strode into the room, coming to sit on the edge of the bed.

'Oh, no, my darling. I'm not making do with that. Amelie deprived me of months of Fleur's life—I might never even have found out that she was born if a mutual friend hadn't told me. I have no intention of going through that again. This time I want everything signed and sealed— legally.'

The painful tears were pushing at the backs of Caitlin's eyes once again and she bent her head to hide them, nervously pleating the sheet over and over in her fingers.

He sounded as if he was discussing some business deal, an important sale in his art-dealing business, not the future of herself and her child—their child. He was cold as ice, clear-headed and totally uninvolved, while her thoughts were fuzzy with weakness and shock, and all her senses were on high alert to the fact that he was there, sitting just inches away.

The sound of his voice was in her ears, the scent of his skin in her nostrils. And in the bright afternoon sunlight that slanted through the window his hair and eyes had a new, almost fierce strength of colour about them, one that brought him stunningly, vividly alive in her mind and in her heart.

But to him, she doubted if she existed as a person. Except as the person who was carrying his precious child.

'So you want me to see a solicitor?' she managed and was stunned when he shook his head again firmly.

'No solicitor,' he declared inflexibly. 'I want this done properly—with a registrar and a priest...'

It took several long, stunned seconds for the truth to dawn on her. Several disturbing moments in which her mind went blank then cleared again, but when she considered what he might really mean she couldn't quite believe it was possible.

'I don't know what you mean.'

'Of course you know damn well what I'm talking about! You're not cutting me out of this child's life, Caitlin!'

She looked as if she'd just received a death sentence rather than a marriage proposal, Rhys reflected ruefully. And no doubt to her it felt very much like that. Probably the only proposal she had ever wanted to hear had been one from her beloved Josh, and that was never going to happen.

And he hadn't exactly *proposed*. Not in the romantic way that he suspected every woman would truly want to be proposed to. But he was in no mood to negotiate. No mood for thinking up niceties and dressing up his feelings in delicate words.

Caitlin was pregnant. Pregnant with a child that this time he knew for sure was his. He wasn't going to risk her keeping that child from him as Amelie had.

Besides, he wanted her to be with him, in his future, so desperately, and he had just been handed the perfect lever with which to manoeuvre her into his life. To tie the knot and have it all signed, sealed and official. And he just hadn't been able to resist grabbing it with both hands.

But if he wasn't careful he might push her into refusing to have anything to do with him ever again—let alone agreeing to be his wife. She was on the edge of doing just that, he knew. It was etched onto her face, clouding the burning golden eyes.

She was about to reject the idea of marriage, or anything. He needed some way of forcing her hand. Something that would buy him her agreement. And then, when she was his wife, maybe, in time, she could come to care for him.

Then he remembered something, something that he prayed might give him the extra edge he needed.

'Hang on a minute,' he muttered, getting to his feet.

Leaving her staring bemusedly after him, he ran down the stairs, collecting something from the hall and making his way back up to the bedroom, where he dumped the bulging suitcase on the floor in full view of the bed.

'So tell me about this,' he said.

He'd hit the right spot; the way her face changed told him that. He wouldn't have thought it was possible for her skin to grow any paler, but when she looked at the case her face became ashen white, her lips almost bloodless.

'I—'

'Where were you planning on going with this?'

Her reply was so soft-voiced and muffled that he couldn't catch it.

'Where?'

'London! And yes, damn you—yes! I *was* coming to see you.'

He struggled not to let the smile that was growing inside escape onto his face. She would only interpret it as triumph and that would ruin everything.

'And why?'

She glared at him the way a wild cat caught in a trap might glare at its captor, knowing all the while that there was no escape.

'I'd thought some more about your—your offer.'

'To look after you and Fleur?'

Her nod was mute and reluctant, her mouth set into a stubborn line.

'You were going to come and live with me in London?'

Again she nodded, still silent, still glaring, though perhaps a little less fiercely.

This time he did let himself smile. The satisfaction was too great to hold it back.

'So what's the difference now? You were going to do it anyway.'

'The difference is—you *know* what the difference is!'

'The difference is the fact that this time I want marriage?'

She didn't need to answer. The look she turned on him said it all.

'But that's how it has to be, Caitlin.'

Deliberately he hardened his voice, needing to drive this home to her so that there could be no possible mistake, no chance of misunderstanding.

'I almost lost Fleur—I'm not going through that again. This baby is my child—and I am going to be its father. Physically, emotionally, legally—I will settle for nothing less.'

Still she resisted him. Her delicate jaw had set stubbornly and her amber eyes burned with defiance, though a little less fiercely than before. Sensing she was weakening, he pressed home his advantage.

'What is it, darling—was my proposal not romantic enough for you? Would you prefer it if I went down on one knee?'

Was that what she had expected Josh to do? Hell, but that rat had hurt her so badly!

'I will do if you want…'

That got to her.

'No!' she said sharply, reaching out a hand as if to stop him if he so much as tried it. 'No! There's no need for that!'

'No,' he agreed. 'We don't have any need for such nonsense, do we? Not when there are two small children—well, one small child and the tiniest beginnings of another—depending on us.'

'But Fleur—what if…?'

She couldn't complete the sentence but she didn't have to. He knew the way that her thoughts were heading without it having to be said.

'I have something for you,' he said, putting a hand into his jacket pocket and pulling out the solicitor's letter, still firmly sealed. 'Here.'

He dropped it on the quilt in front of her, watching fixedly as she reached out slowly, picked it up, then turned to him with a bewildered frown on her face.

'The DNA test results,' he told her, his voice not quite as steady as he would have liked. 'I've never opened it so I have no idea what it says. But it doesn't matter now.'

'It doesn't?' Her voice was little more than a croak.

'Not if you'll marry me. Fleur is who she is, Caitlin. And I love her for what she is. Her parentage won't change that one way or another. If you marry me, she'll be ours. Our daughter—our child, the same as the one you're carrying inside you. We'll be a family together.'

He paused, swallowing to ease the dryness of his mouth, as he ran an uneasy hand through his hair, praying she wouldn't see the way his fingers shook.

'Maybe one day, some time in the future, Fleur will

need—or want—to know. So I'm asking you to keep that safe for her in case she ever asks for it. But I don't want to see it. I'll never ask. It doesn't matter any more.'

'That's—that's…'

Whatever she had been about to say was choked off as she crushed the envelope tight in her hand. A moment later she turned to him and her eyes were brilliant with unshed tears.

'Rhys…'

But he couldn't wait any longer. Couldn't stand here in doubt, halfway between heaven and hell. He had to know. He had to have her answer before his mind totally blew a fuse.

'Caitlin, say yes! Say you'll marry me. There are two children who need us.'

'You want me to marry you—for the babies' sakes?'

'For the babies' sakes.'

If that was what it took, then he'd go along with it. For now.

'Can you think of a better reason?'

Yes, Caitlin thought. Oh, yes. I can think of a much better reason. The one where you say you love me. That you can't live without me. That you want me with you for the rest of your life. Children or no children. For richer, for poorer. In sickness and in health. Till death us do part.

But that sort of proposal from Rhys would only ever happen in her dreams. 'For the babies' sakes' was the only thing she was going to get.

And she had to say yes or no.

And he wasn't going to take no for an answer.

And so:

'For the babies' sakes, then yes,' she said.

CHAPTER FOURTEEN

'WELL, Cait...'

Bob Richardson turned to his daughter, who stood beside him in the porch of the small village church looking stunningly beautiful but almost as pale as the lovely white dress and veil she wore.

'Are you ready, love?'

'Ready,' Caitlin managed, even producing a weak smile, though inside she knew the truth was that she was very far from ready.

How could she be 'ready' for this wedding?

Oh, she was dressed in all her finery—the finery that Rhys had insisted on, rejecting without hesitation her tentative suggestion for a secret wedding, a purely civil ceremony. Her make-up was immaculate, her hair scooped up into an elegant arrangement under the circle of fresh flowers—ivory roses and tiny stephanotis—that held her delicate veil in place. Her bouquet was made up of the same blooms and she knew that beyond the heavy wooden door the cool interior of the church was decorated with them too.

But would she ever be emotionally ready for a marriage that had nothing of love in it but only convenience and the fact that she had unexpectedly fallen pregnant to the man who was to become her husband?

'We're doing this thing properly!' Rhys had insisted when she'd protested that there was no need to go to any trouble to arrange the ceremony. 'It will be perfect right down to the very last detail. Every flower, every hymn, every candle will be just as you've always dreamed of it. I want it to be your day.'

But how could it be perfect when the only thing that could make it that way was for her to have Rhys's love? When all that she wanted was to know he'd given his heart to her as she'd given hers to him? That love was all that she needed to make her day perfect. With it she would want for nothing else, and without it nothing could ever redeem a day that should be so wonderfully happy and yet was so desperately, terribly empty.

But her father was waiting for her. Beyond the doors, the organist was coming to the end of the third repetition of the Bach sonata he had been playing, and she knew that the congregation would be starting to get restless. She was already a few minutes late.

'Cait?'

Bob's gentle prompting pulled her from her melancholy thoughts and brought her back to reality.

There was no way this wedding could ever be perfect. But it was the only wedding she was going to get, and she had promised Rhys that she would be here—for the babies' sakes.

Drawing in a deep breath, she squared her shoulders and forced a brief, bright—at least she hoped it looked bright—smile.

'Ready as I'll ever be.'

She took the seconds while her father pulled the transparent veil down over her face and arranged it carefully to let her fingers rest very lightly on the spot under her white silk gown where the baby—Rhys's baby—was lying. A tiny speck of life at the moment, but one that had had such a huge impact on her life, changing it forever.

He'll be a good father to you, she promised secretly, knowing deep in her heart that that, at least, was true.

Seeing Rhys with Fleur, how could she ever doubt that he would be a wonderful parent to this new baby as he already was to the little girl? He might never know if he was her biological father or not, but there was so much more to being a father than simply starting off the miracle of life.

And in every aspect of fathering, Rhys just couldn't be faulted.

'Let's get this show on the road.'

Her father beamed his pride at her as he held out his arm. Grateful for his support, knowing that her legs were faintly unsteady beneath her, Caitlin tucked her hand under it and made herself step forward into the cool nave of the church.

The traditional sound of the *Wedding March* swung around her. The rich scent of the flowers and the burning candles swirled in the air, making her still delicate stomach protest faintly. But she just held on tighter to her father and paced slowly and elegantly towards the beautifully decorated altar.

The curtain of the veil that came down in front of her face had an effect as if a soft mist were hovering before her eyes, blurring some faces as she passed and making them indistinct. But there was one person she saw sharply and clearly. One tall, powerful, masculine frame, one proudly carried head of rich dark hair that drew her gaze and held it. And once she had looked that way it was as if there was no one else in the whole church except for Rhys. The man who was going to be her husband.

He stood straight and strong at the foot of the altar steps, his dark suit fitting perfectly to every gorgeous inch, his feet planted firmly on the stone-flagged floor as if stating his perfect right to be there.

Not for Rhys the feel of trembling legs, the nervous blurring of eyesight. He needed no physical support from the friend who was his best man, no one to lean on in the way that Caitlin was leaning on her father now.

Rhys had no doubt as to what he was doing here and why. He wanted nothing more from this wedding than what he was getting and he was quite content with that. He was marrying her 'for the babies' sakes' and only for that.

Well, perhaps not *only* for that. He had made it plain that the blazing sexual passion that had hurried them into bed so precipitately and unguardedly was a bonus that he welcomed in what was otherwise a marriage of convenience. He showed quite openly that he desired her with a force that could barely be held in check until after the wedding was over. That as much as anything had been the reason for the rush to the altar, just a few short weeks after his unromantic proposal. He didn't care if people guessed about the baby, or started counting on their fingers when she began to show.

'I can't wait to have you in my bed every night,' he'd told her, his voice husky and raw with need. 'Can't wait to have my ring on your finger and to be able to truly say that you are mine.'

Well, that was one thing that they agreed on, Caitlin reflected, unable to restrain the faint smile of delight that always touched her lips when she thought of the physical ecstasy that Rhys's lovemaking always brought. She was as impatient for him as he was for her.

That part of their marriage at least would prove no hardship at all.

They had reached the end of the aisle. Her father eased his supporting arm away; the bridesmaid stepped forward and took the bouquet from her. And Caitlin turned slowly to face the man who was to be her husband.

Rhys had tried to stand facing the altar, as he knew he was expected to. He had tried not to look over his shoulder to see Caitlin walking down the aisle towards him. But he had been unable to stop himself from doing so.

For one thing, she had been late. Ten whole minutes late. Ten long, nerve-racking, mind-numbing, panic-inducing minutes. And, although he knew that traditionally it was the bride's prerogative to be a little late for her wedding, he had found the time spent waiting for her to arrive, waiting and wondering *if* she was going to arrive, had almost destroyed his composure.

And when at last the whisper that his bride was here had filtered into the church and through the congregation, reaching him like the flow of a wave onto the shore, he had known such a rush of relief that he could only nod at the smiling celebrant, unable to find the strength to say a word.

He had stood as instructed, fixing his eyes on the flame of a candle burning a few yards away, staring at it until it became just a golden blur, with no edge or definition to it. And staring had helped him stay still and straight, not giving in to the clenching of his stomach, the dryness of his mouth.

And now she was here. Now she stood beside him, silent and still, and ethereal in the beautiful white dress, her lovely face partly hidden by the veil she wore. Only those huge, luminous eyes shone clearly visible behind the fine material. The rest of her face was so pale he could hardly see it.

Nerves, he decided. And no surprise. He felt bad enough for two.

'Hi,' he whispered, flashing her a quick smile in the hope of making her relax.

She didn't smile back in response. She just looked up into his face with those wide golden eyes in a way that only added to his already unsettled state.

God, he couldn't wait until this formality and fuss was

over. Then he could take her away on the honeymoon he had planned and they could relax together. Just the two of them, and Fleur. And then, out of sight of prying eyes and in the privacy he craved, he could start to show her how he felt.

They could start their married life as he meant to go on, and maybe, just maybe, he could also start to win her round too.

'Soon be done,' he whispered encouragingly.

He reached for the hand that hung at her side, folding his fingers firmly around it. There was no response, but she didn't pull away either. She just let her hand lie in his grasp, limp and unresisting, not answering his squeeze of her fingers with her own.

'Ready?' the priest asked, and Rhys nodded firmly.

'Go ahead.'

Ready?

There was that question again, Caitlin thought. The one she couldn't answer.

She was ready to marry Rhys. She had never been more ready for anything in her life—if only he loved her. And Rhys was ready for—for what? Ready to become a father. And to take her on as his wife, if that was what it took to achieve his aim.

What was it he had said?

Soon be done.

He wanted this wedding over and done with so that he could get the pretence of love and dreams and happy-ever-after out of the way and they could start the sort of marriage he really wanted. The one where she had his children and he got what he wanted.

'Do you, Rhys Matthew…?'

Vaguely she heard the priest begin the lead-in to their

marriage vows and, although she tried to concentrate, her thoughts swam in a sudden panic of rejection.

How could she stand here and listen to Rhys tell everyone that he would love and honour her when she knew it was a lie?

How could she let him promise to care for and feel for her when she knew that no such thoughts or feelings were in his heart?

How could she let herself down by going into a relationship that denied her everything she had ever hoped for and dreamed of, and believed in?

And yet how could she not go through with it when Fleur and her own baby's futures were involved?

She had to go through with it.

For the babies' sakes.

'Caitlin Marie…' the priest had turned to her '…do you take this man, Rhys Matthew…?'

Panic was a dancing haze before her eyes. A sound that seemed like the buzz of a thousand frantic bees sounded in her ears, drowning out his words.

Rhys must have said 'I do', and she hadn't heard it.

He must have said 'I do', and sounded as if he meant it.

But she knew that it was not the truth. That it had never been the truth. That…

'No!'

The word was a cry of panic, of rejection, of despair, breaking into the priest's words and shocking him and the whole congregation into silence.

She felt Rhys's sudden stillness. Sensed him turn towards her, blue eyes very dark.

'No!' she said again. 'I'm sorry—so sorry—but I can't— I can't!'

And, gathering up the long silken skirts of her dress, she whirled away from him. Away from the altar and the priest's stunned expression. Away down the aisle, past the staring, bewildered congregation. Away out into the bright summer sunlight, hearing the heavy wooden door slam shut behind her.

No?

Rhys just couldn't believe what had happened. What he'd heard.

Had he heard right?

Had Caitlin truly said no?

He was turning to her, to stare, to question, to—he didn't know what he was going to do, but she had already gone. She had gathered up the skirts of her dress in both hands and was running away, down the aisle, like Cinderella fleeing from the ball on the stroke of midnight.

She'd even lost one of her shoes in her headlong flight.

She'd gone. Left him.

Left him standing at the altar in the middle of their wedding.

The silence in the church was so intense that it was painful to his ears. He could see the entire congregation—friends, family, his and hers—everyone was staring, watching, wondering.

Wondering how he would react to this very public humiliation.

Caitlin had left him. Jilted him. And he had no idea in hell why.

There was a nervous cough, a faint movement. Caitlin's father, getting up from his seat to go after his daughter.

'No!'

It was the roar of a wounded lion. A lion who didn't know if the pain inflicted on him would ultimately prove fatal and quite frankly didn't care. He was staking out his territory, declaring that *he* was in charge here.

'No!' he said again. 'Leave this to me! It's me she ran

out on. And I'm the one who has to deal with this. I'm the one who has to go after her.'

I'm the one who has to go after her. The words repeated over and over in his head as he strode down the aisle in Caitlin's footsteps, snatching up the delicate satin shoe as he went. The one who has to go after her and find out just what's going on. The one who has to face whatever she has to say, even if it was only a repetition of that hateful 'No!' A declaration that she would never, ever marry him.

That she still loved Joshua Hewland, damn him, and would always be faithful to his memory.

And he would have to accept that if it was what she truly wanted. He couldn't force her into something she would regret for the rest of her life.

And that was when he knew that he'd really got it bad. That as well as losing his heart, he'd lost what passed for his mind as well. And given them both into the care of the woman who'd just run in headlong flight away from him.

The sunlight outside was brilliant, blinding and hot after the cool, shadowy light of the interior of the church. For a few worrying seconds he stood, blinking hard, his hand up against his eyes to shield him from the glare, struggling to see.

And then, at last, he found her.

She hadn't been able to go far. With only one shoe and hampered by the elegant dress, she had only managed to get partway across the churchyard to where a small stone bench stood in the shade of a huge oak tree. And there she sat, huddled in a corner, her face turned away from him, looking impossibly small, impossibly delicate, impossibly forlorn.

And it was the 'forlorn' that gave him hope.

If she had truly wanted never to marry him—if she wanted nothing more than to be free, to get away from him and live her life without him, then now she would feel relief, the sense of a weight lifted from her shoulders. She would be scared of the future, with the baby on the way, apprehensive about how she would cope.

But she would never be forlorn.

Not his Caitlin. His strong, brave, caring, coping Caitlin. The Caitlin who had seen her fiancé betray her and move in with another woman. Who had taken that other woman's child in and cared for it as her own, not caring if it had been the result of her own betrayal. Who had fought like a tiger to defend that baby.

And who finally had been prepared to let Fleur go, no matter how much it might have pained her, if the baby was to be with her real father.

'Caitlin…'

Her head jerked up at the sound of her name. She half turned, then looked away again, staring past him, golden eyes still hidden by that ridiculous veil, fixed on space. Unseeingly, he was sure.

'Go away!'

It was fierce, but not strong. The sound of someone who was determined to say something, and by sheer force of will-power kept their voice level and clear.

So he dismissed it easily.

'No,' he said. 'I won't go away. Not until we've talked this through.'

'There's nothing to talk about.'

She kept her face stubbornly averted, even when he came and sat beside her on the weathered stone bench.

'I think there's plenty to talk about,' he insisted. 'Like why you ever came here in the first place if you didn't mean to marry me. Why you got as far as the altar. Why—'

'I thought I could!'

She flung it at him in desperation, wanting only to shut

him up. She had never dreamed that he would come after her. Had prayed that he would be so shocked, so furious at the way she had publicly humiliated him, that he would stay right where he was, never wanting to see her again.

'I thought I could go through with it—OK? I came here to marry you as I promised. I came to say my vows and sign the registry. To arrive here as Miss Caitlin Richardson and leave as Mrs Caitlin Morgan!'

And be so, so proud to have his name as her own.

'I meant to do it!'

'So why didn't you?'

'I couldn't. When it came to the point, I couldn't go through with it. I couldn't promise to honour and l-love when…when…'

'When what, Caitlin?' he asked when she faltered, swallowing down the words with the tears that were streaming over her cheeks, soaking into the veil. 'Tell me.'

Oh, what harm could it do now? No doubt he had guessed anyway. Why else would she have run from the church rather than go through with a marriage she had already agreed to on the terms he offered?

'When it wasn't true! When it would all have been a lie!'

'What?'

To her horror, his hands closed over her shoulders, bringing her round to face him.

'What would have been a lie?'

But she didn't have the courage to repeat the words. Biting her lip hard, she could only shake her head, unable to answer him.

'Caitlin…'

With a gentleness that twisted in her heart, Rhys took both sides of the lacy veil in his hands and lifted it carefully away from her face, folding it back over the coronet of flowers. Blinking hard in the cruelly brilliant sunlight, she could only pray that he would take the sheen in her eyes as being caused by the blinding effect of its brightness.

'Oh, Caitlin.'

Her heart stopped in shock as she felt the delicate pressure of his mouth on her face, kissing away the trails of the tears, caressing her skin...

'I always knew,' he murmured against her cheek.

'Kn-knew what?'

'That you don't love me. That your love was given to Joshua all the time. It doesn't matter. I have enough for both of us.'

She really had to be hearing things. The sun had to have affected her brain. She was hearing things that just weren't true. Things that she dreamed of, longed for.

But things that just couldn't be happening.

She shook her head in a desperate attempt to clear her thoughts and saw him smile in a way that she could only describe as resigned—and terribly sad.

'I don't ask for you to love me back. I'll never ask for that, if it's something you can't give me. If you'll just be in my life so that I can see you, care for you, love you with all my heart, I won't even ask for marriage if that's something you can't give.'

'L-love...'

She had to say it, though she knew it couldn't be right. She wasn't hearing what she thought he was saying. So she had to ask.

'Are you saying that you *love* me?'

He actually laughed, though there was a strained, ragged edge to it.

'What else do you think I'm saying, my love? Why else do you think I asked you to marry me?'

'For—for the babies' sakes. No?' she questioned as he shook his dark head.

'No—well, yes. Yes, if marrying me for the babies' sakes was the only reason you would say yes. But also because I love you...I more than love you—I adore you. I was so desperate to keep you with me that I would have taken any way out; any way that would get you to promise to be with me, live with me...'

'Love you?' Caitlin inserted softly and saw him close his eyes briefly in an expression of such immeasurable longing that it tore at her already tender heart.

'I wish!' he said fervently.

And there was only one answer she could give him.

'Your wish is granted.'

His lids flew up, brilliant, bewildered, blue eyes blazing into hers, endless questions in their depths.

'Cait?'

Leaning forward, she pressed her hand against his cheek, looked deep into his eyes and smiled with all the love that was in her heart.

'I love you,' she said slowly and confidently. 'There— is that clear enough for you? I love you with all my heart. It was never truly love I felt for Josh—I see that now. Now that I know what loving you feels like. When I know how deep and strong and perfect love can be.'

'Oh, *Cait*!'

He gathered her into his arms. Kissed her hard with all the love and the longing and the need that she had seen in his face. But then, just as she wanted to kiss him back, he stopped her, very gently.

'Wait.'

And as she watched, bewildered, he eased himself away from her, moved from the stone seat and went down on one knee on the grass before her.

Taking her hand in his, he held it while he looked up into her face, his love, his devotion open there for her to see.

'Caitlin, my love, my life, will you marry me, here and now? In front of everyone? Will you let me tell you how much I love you? Let me promise to care for you, honour you all the rest of my life. Please, my darling. Please tell me that you will be my wife—for my sake and mine alone.'

There was only one answer she could give him and words were not enough. So she answered him with a kiss that held all her heart inside it.

And after a few more sun-soaked, private, loving moments there in the quiet churchyard, she let him slip her shoe back onto her foot and lift her to her feet.

And then, with the strength of his hand in hers and his love in her heart, she went back into the church with him, knowing that now she could repeat her vows with all the joy and honesty and trust that she was capable of feeling because she had no doubts at all that they both meant them and that they were an expression of a love that would last for all of their lifetimes.

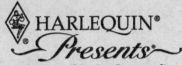

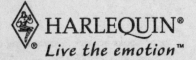

If you enjoyed what you just read,
then we've got an offer you can't resist!

Take 2 bestselling love stories FREE!

Plus get a FREE surprise gift!